DATE DUE

AUG 3 1			
MAY 1 3			
			PRINTED IN U.S.A.

NORSE MYTHS

A VIKING GRAPHIC NOVEL

THOR AND LOKI

by CARL BOWEN and TOD SMITH and REX LOKUS

STONE ARCH BOOKS
a capstone imprint

Norse Myths is published by Stone Arch Books
A Capstone Imprint
1710 Roe Crest Drive
North Mankato, Minnesota 56003
www.mycapstone.com

Cataloging-in-Publication Data is available at the Library of Congress website.
ISBN: 978-1-4965-3490-3 (hardcover)
ISBN: 978-1-4965-3494-1 (paperback)
ISBN: 978-1-4965-3498-9 (eBook PDF)

Summary: Loki, the god of mischief, is Thor's troublesome adopted brother. Odin, their father (and ruler of the Viking gods), orders the quarrelsome siblings to tame the violent Giants once and for all together. But what Loki and Thor find in their series of adventures puts them in conflict with each other as well as with the giants. And in the land of Utgard, a mysterious place made from magic and illusion, Thor must trust his magic-wielding and misbehaving brother in order to get out alive. Likewise, Loki must count on his brother's unmatched strength if he hopes to survive their encounters with the Giants.

Editor: Aaron Sautter
Designer: Kristi Carlson
Production Specialist: Laura Manthe

Printed in the United States of America.
009624F16

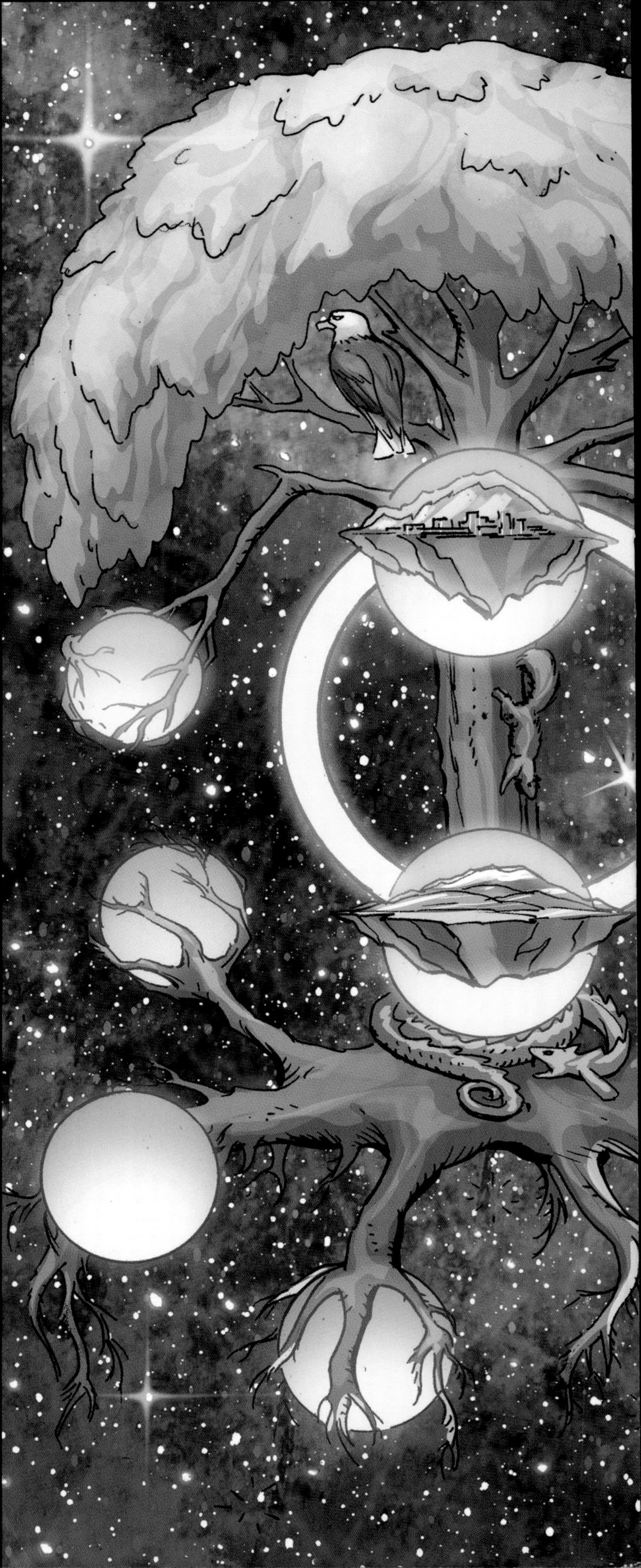

TABLE OF CONTENTS

UNEASY ALLIES

The Aesir (AY-zir) were the gods of the ancient Norse people. From their heavenly realm of Asgard, they ruled over the world of mortals and the lands of the dead. The Norse gods had one major enemy—the giants who lived in the land called Jötunheim (YOH-toon-heym).

To make peace with the giants, Odin, the wise ruler of the Aesir, agreed to raise a giant child as his own son. The child, Loki, has made a name for himself as a trickster and a troublemaker. Fortunately, he uses his sly cunning more often in the Aesir's favor than against his adopted family.

Loki's main rival is Odin's son, Thor. Where Loki is quick and clever, Thor is proud, brave, and strong. Wielding his magical war hammer, Thor is happiest when he's smashing Asgard's enemies into dust. However, Thor is quick to anger and would prefer to rid the Nine Worlds of Asgard's foes once and for all.

Wise Odin forces his two sons to work together at every opportunity, knowing that only they can keep each other in check. He hopes their example can teach the peoples of Asgard and Jötunheim how to live in peace despite their differences.

Assuming that Thor and Loki don't kill each other first ...

THE MAIN PLAYERS

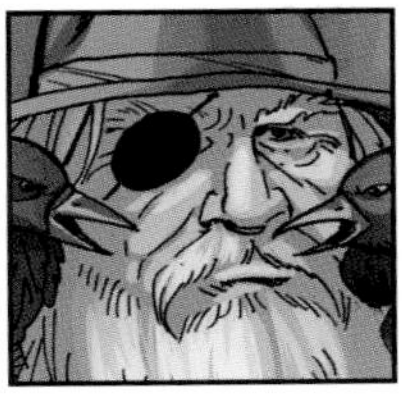

Odin—the one-eyed All-Father and wise ruler of the Norse gods. Odin is the god of many things, including healing, sorcery, battle, and poetry. He values wisdom and knowledge above all.

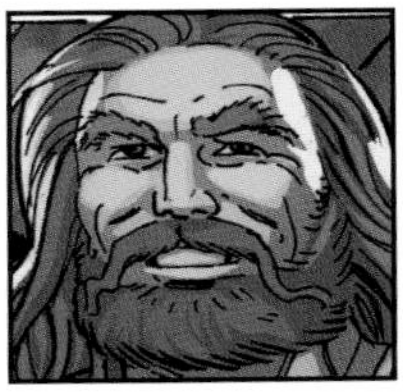

Thor—the redheaded, quick-tempered son of Odin. He is the Norse god of thunder, lightning, and strength. With his magical war hammer, Mjölnir (MYOHL-neer), Thor can call lightning from the sky to defend Asgard from all its enemies.

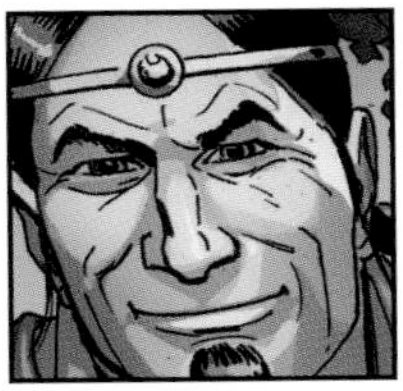

Loki—a small giant and blood brother to the gods. A clever shape-shifter, Loki enjoys tricking the Norse gods. He resents them, but he assists them when it suits his purposes. He can solve almost any problem through his wits and cunning.

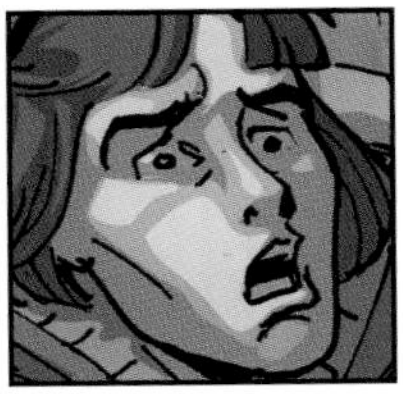

Thialfi—a young manservant to Thor. The mortal son of a simple farmer, Thialfi is tricked into disobeying Thor's orders. To make amends he accompanies and helps the Norse god during his adventures.

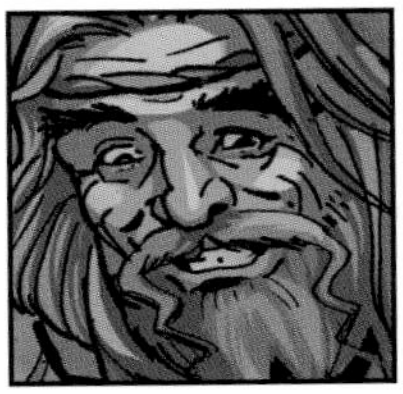

Skrymir—a truly massive giant that Thor, Loki, and Thialfi meet on the road to Jötunheim. He is so large they mistake one of his gloves as a cave. He seems friendly, but appearances can be deceiving.

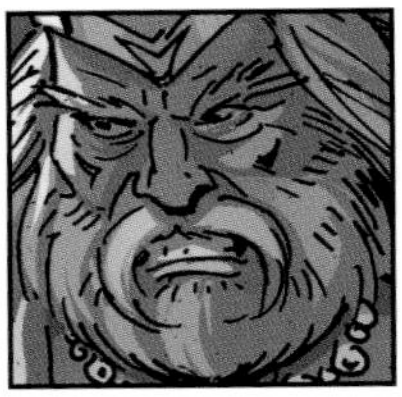

Utgarda-Loki—the cruel and clever giant king of Utgard, a stronghold on the river Ifing. When the Aesir enter the giants' lands, Utgarda-Loki uses his cunning and magic to make sure the Norse gods don't cause trouble.

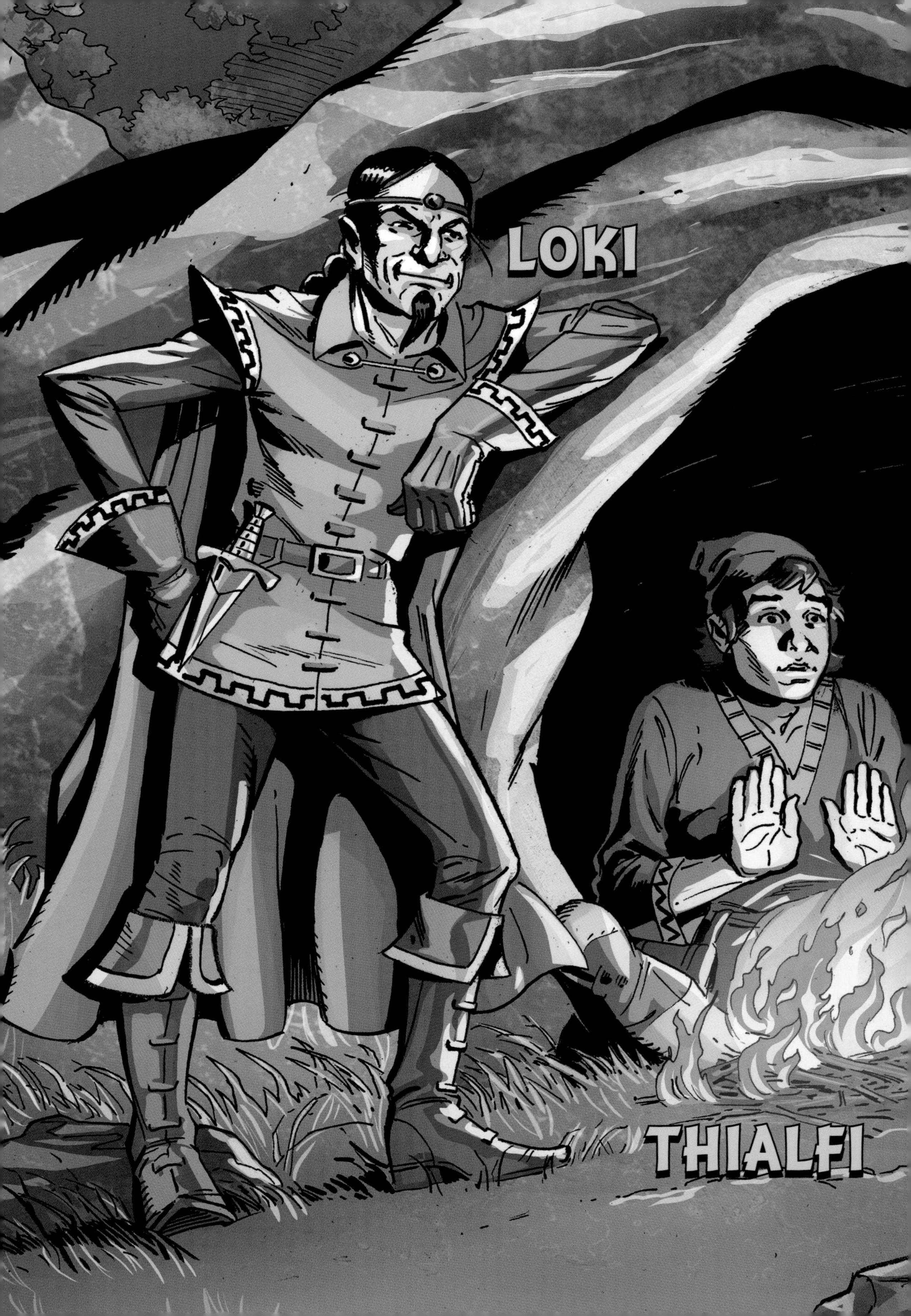
LOKI
THIALFI

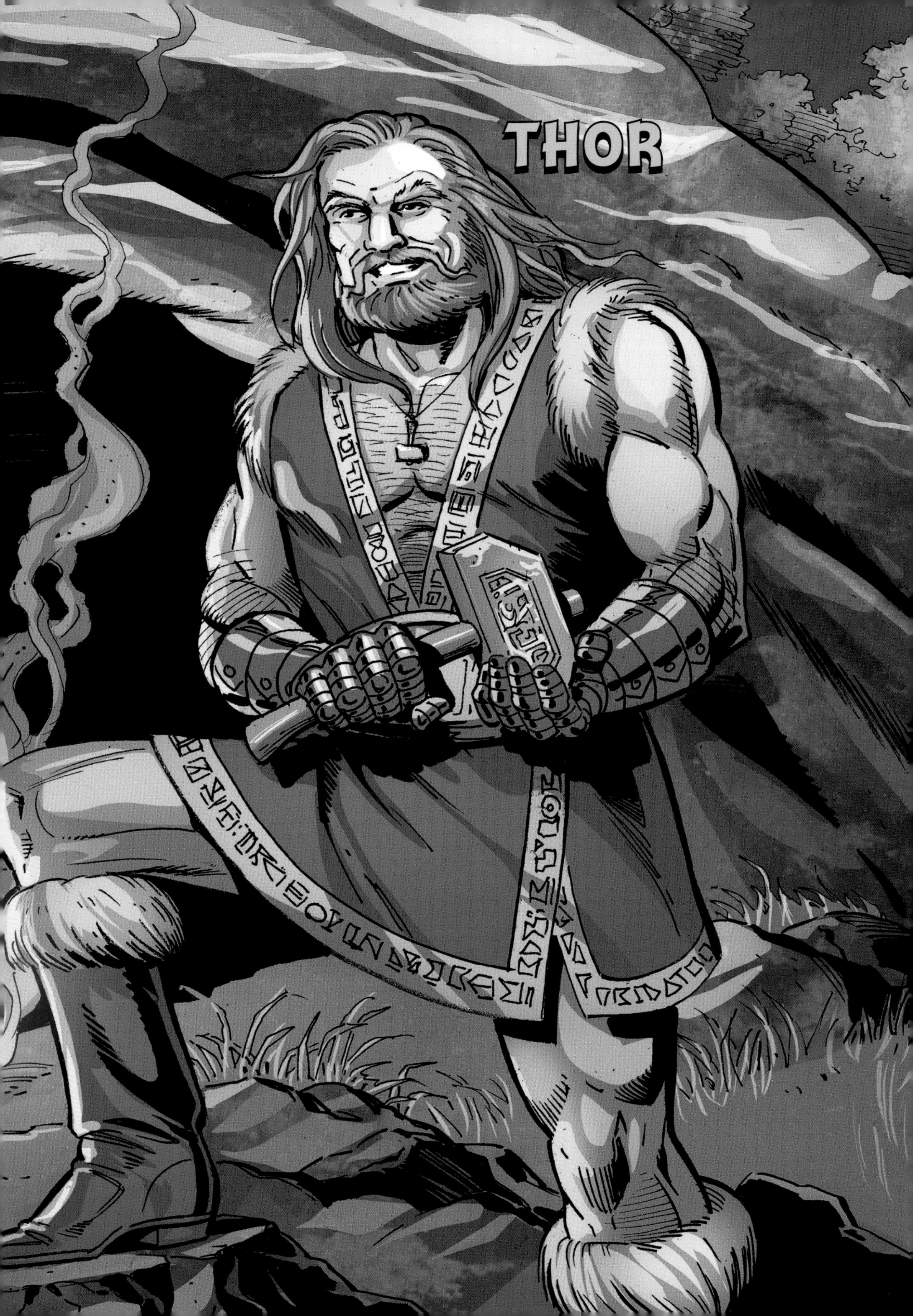
THOR

CHAPTER 1
LOOKING FOR ADVENTURE

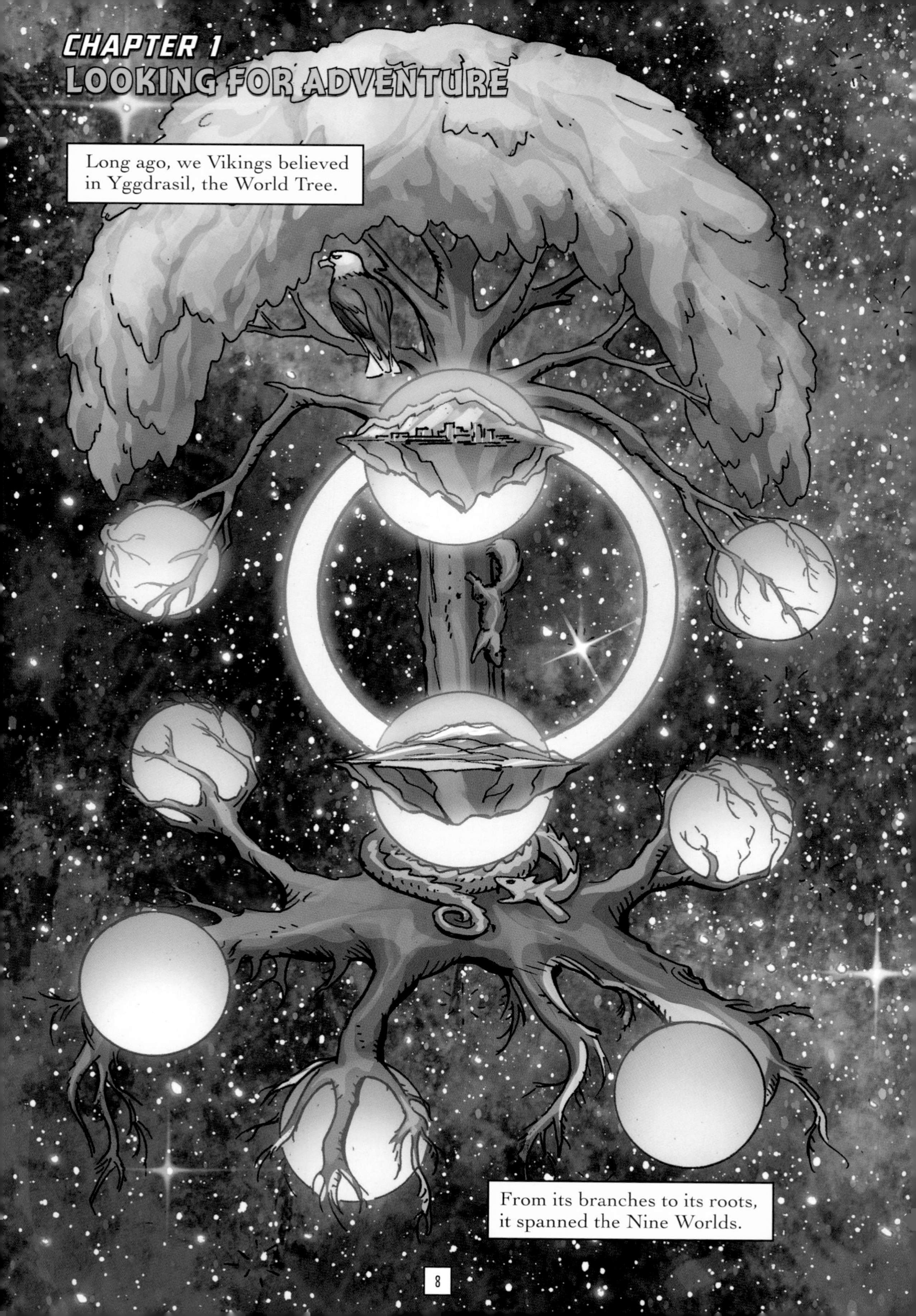
Long ago, we Vikings believed in Yggdrasil, the World Tree.
From its branches to its roots, it spanned the Nine Worlds.

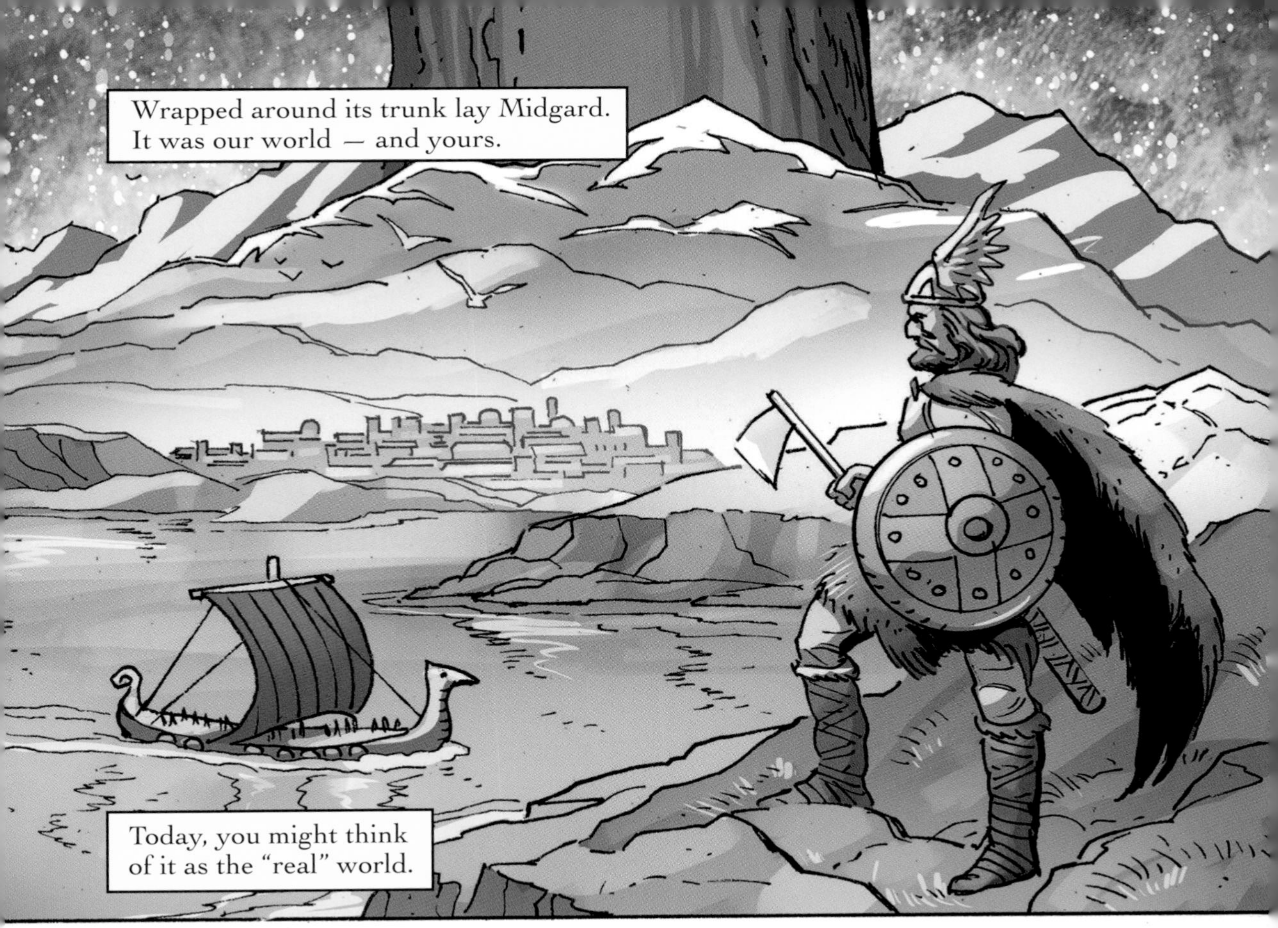
Wrapped around its trunk lay Midgard.
It was our world — and yours.
Today, you might think of it as the "real" world.

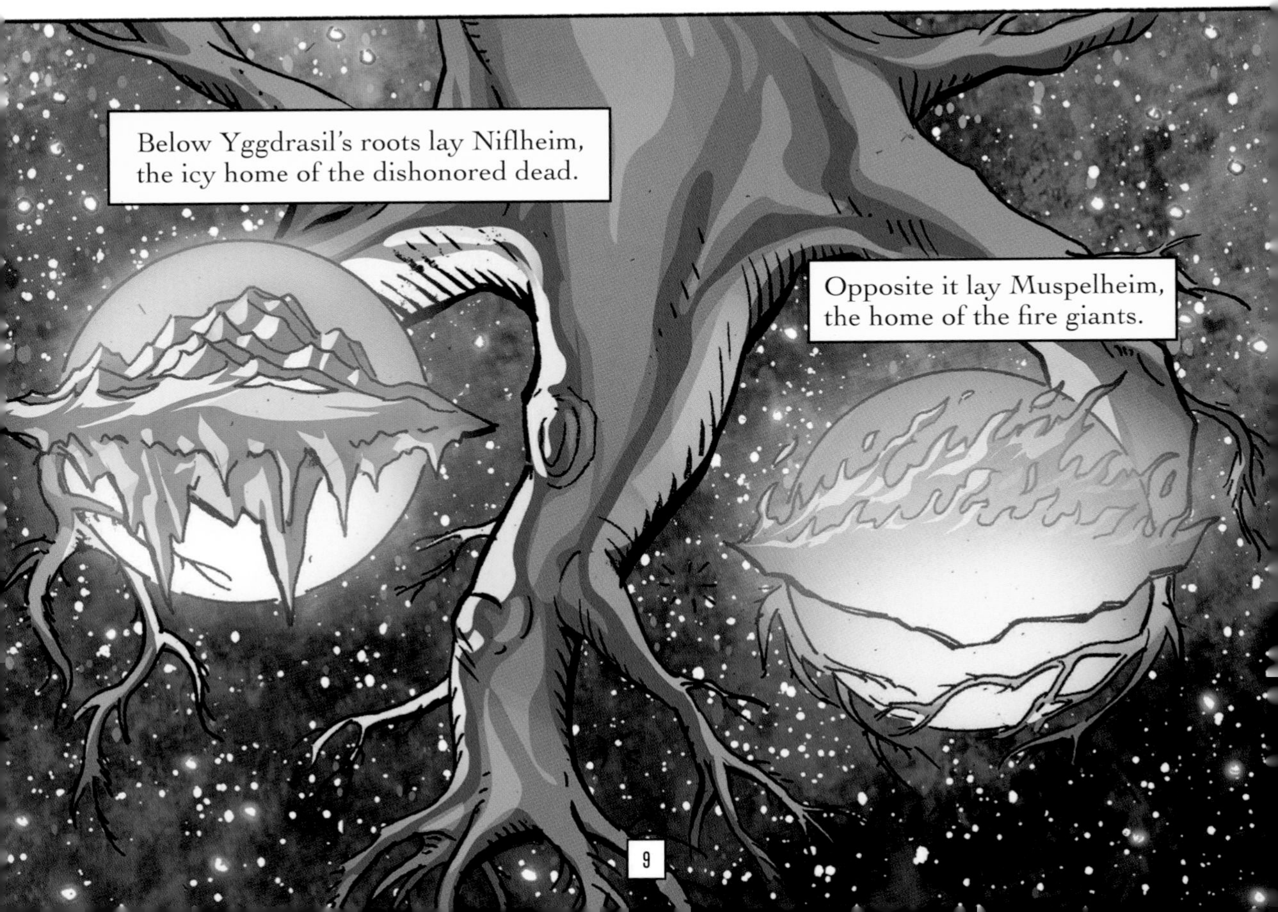
Below Yggdrasil's roots lay Niflheim, the icy home of the dishonored dead.
Opposite it lay Muspelheim, the home of the fire giants.

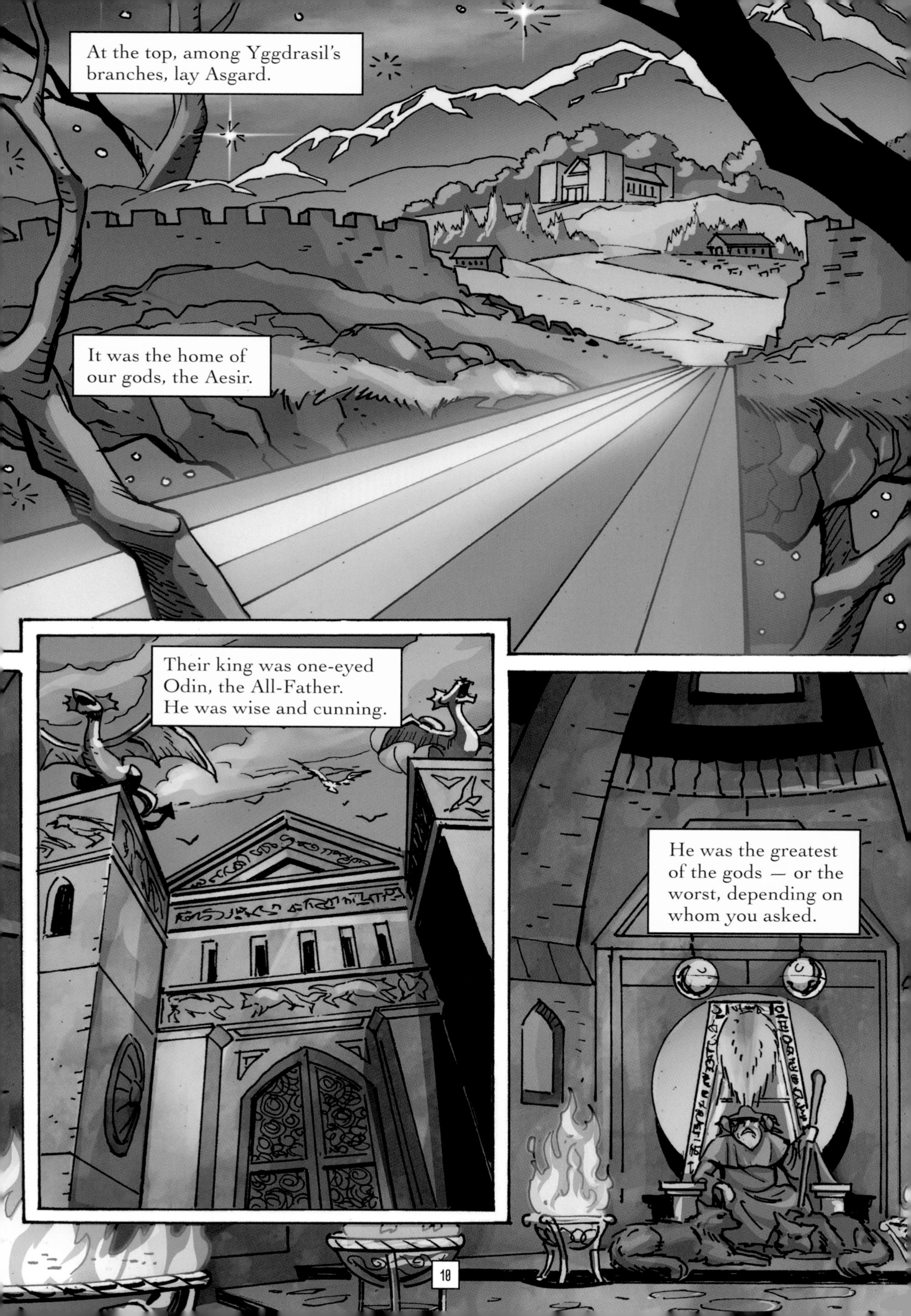
At the top, among Yggdrasil's branches, lay Asgard.
It was the home of our gods, the Aesir.
Their king was one-eyed Odin, the All-Father. He was wise and cunning.
He was the greatest of the gods — or the worst, depending on whom you asked.

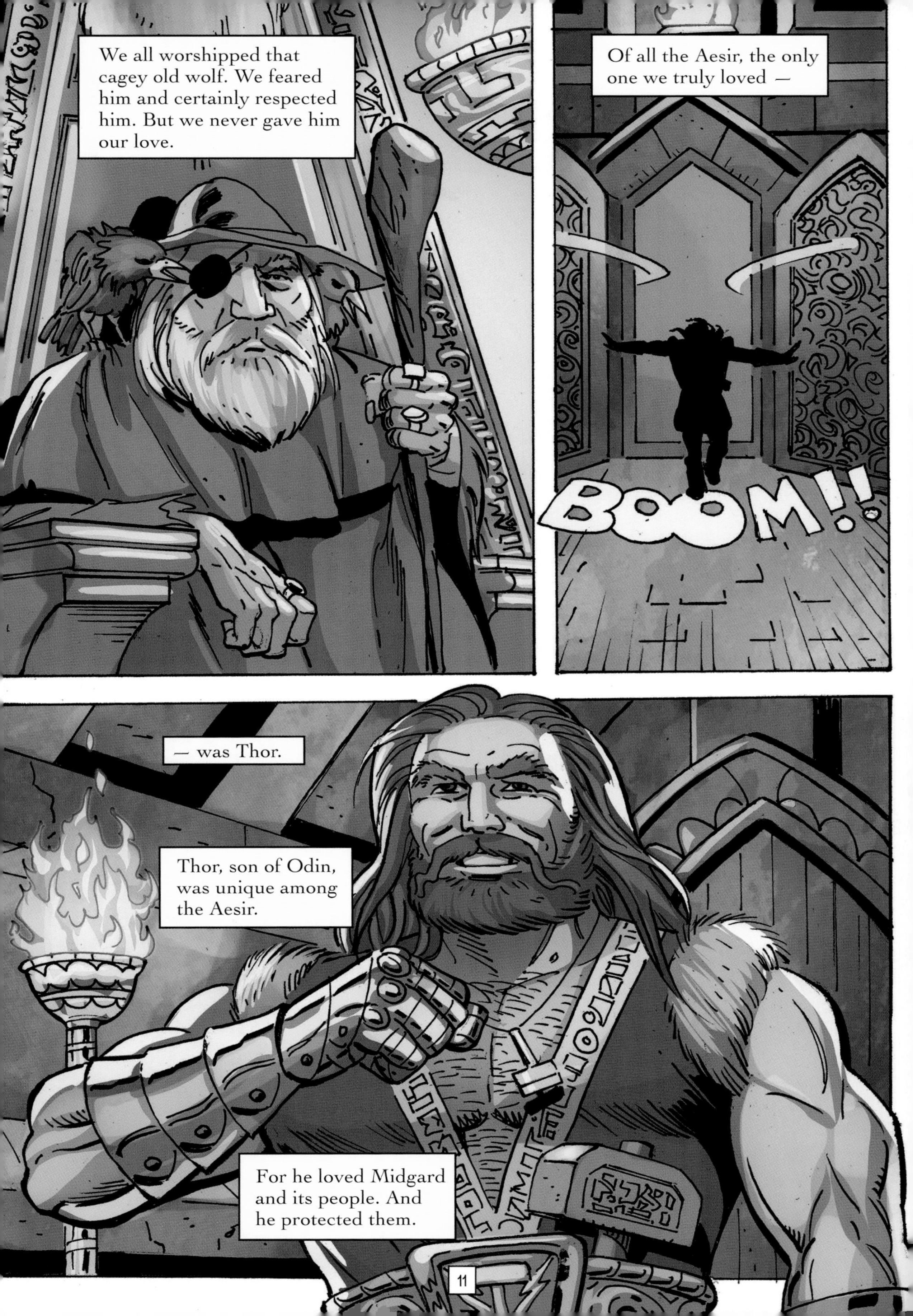
We all worshipped that cagey old wolf. We feared him and certainly respected him. But we never gave him our love.
Of all the Aesir, the only one we truly loved —
BOOM!!
— was Thor.
Thor, son of Odin, was unique among the Aesir.
For he loved Midgard and its people. And he protected them.

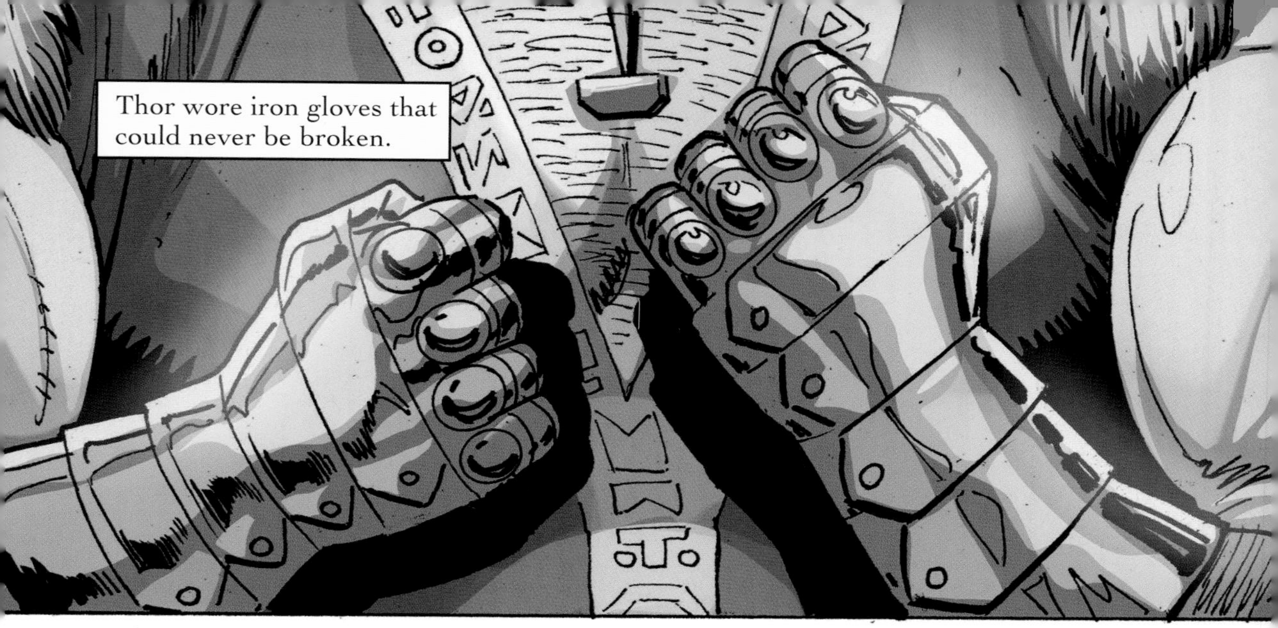
Thor wore iron gloves that could never be broken.

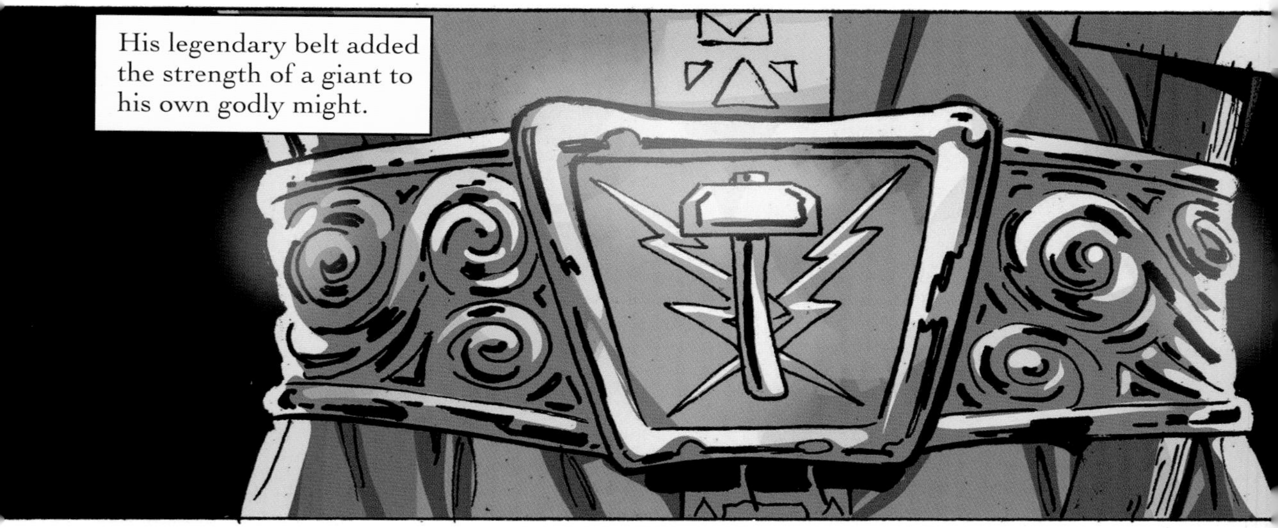
His legendary belt added the strength of a giant to his own godly might.

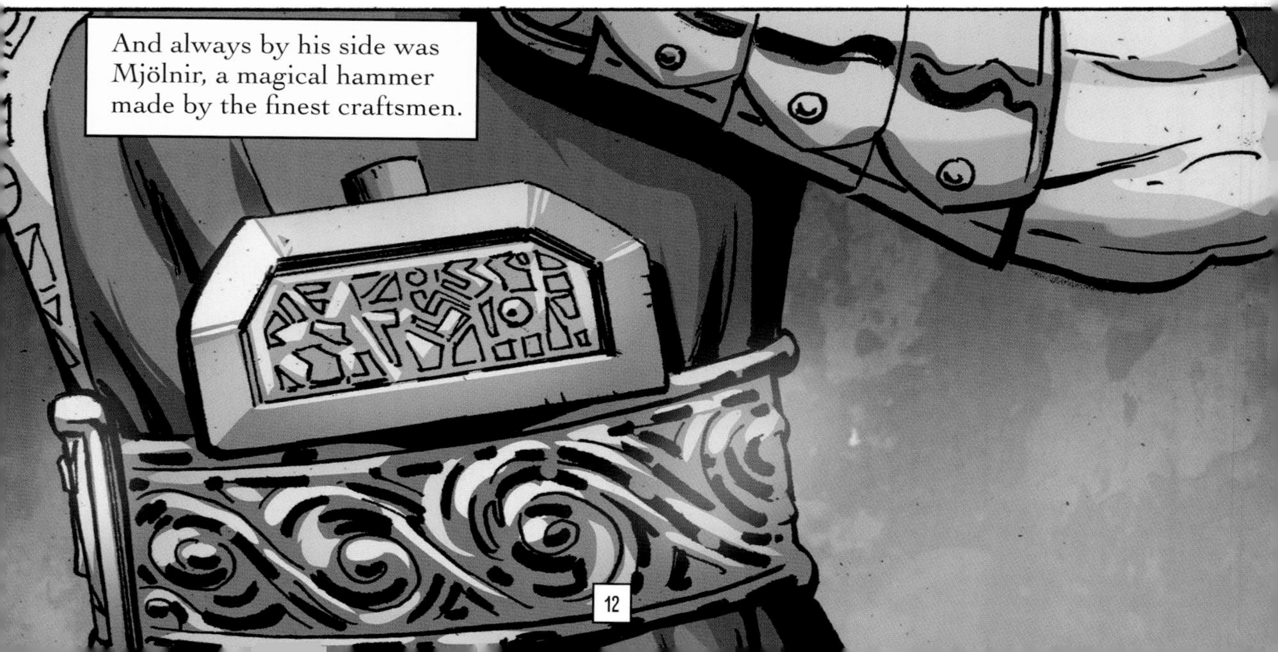
And always by his side was Mjölnir, a magical hammer made by the finest craftsmen.

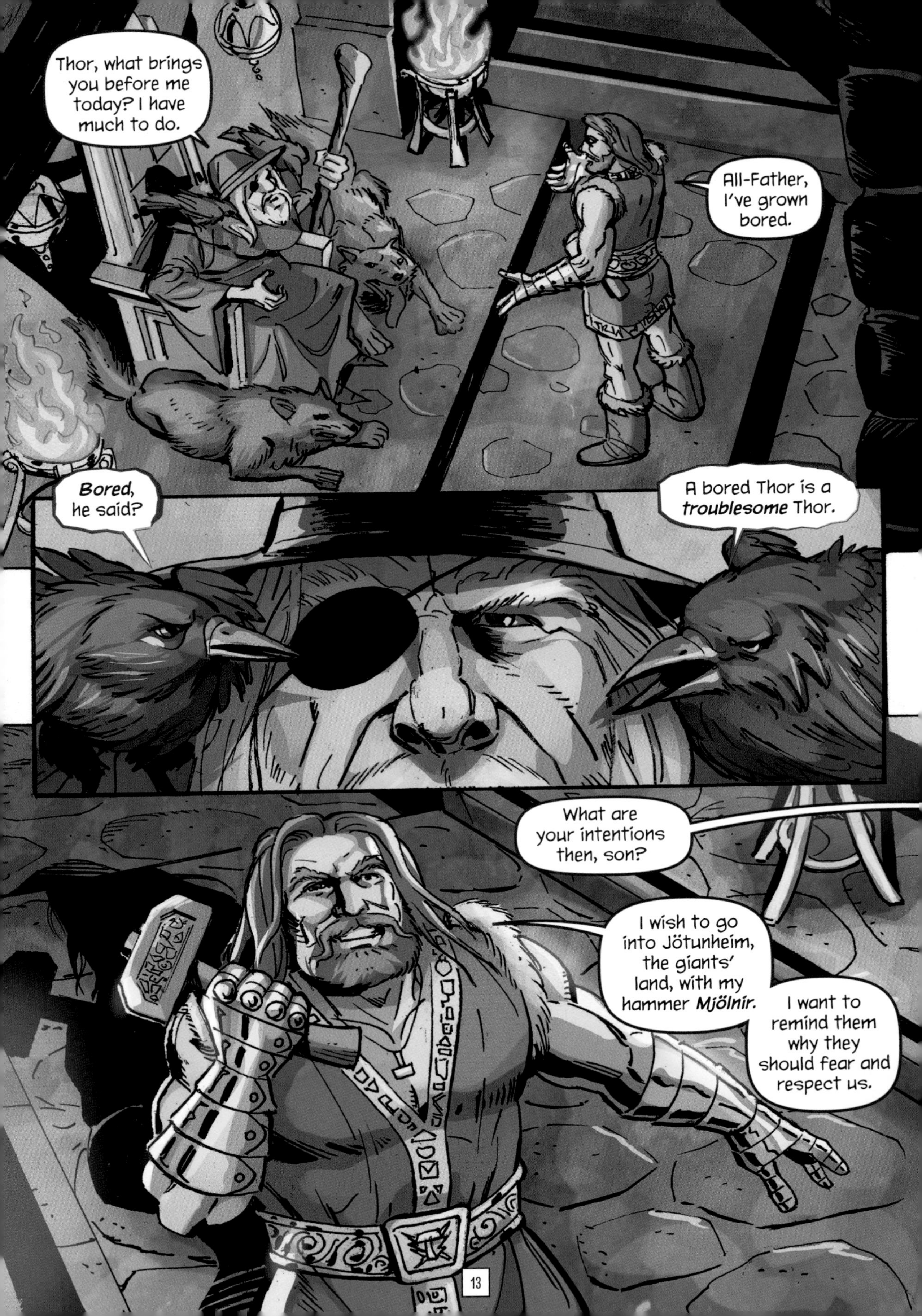
Thor, what brings you before me today? I have much to do.
All-Father, I've grown bored.
Bored, he said?
A bored Thor is a *troublesome* Thor.
What are your intentions then, son?
I wish to go into Jötunheim, the giants' land, with my hammer *Mjölnir*.
I want to remind them why they should fear and respect us.

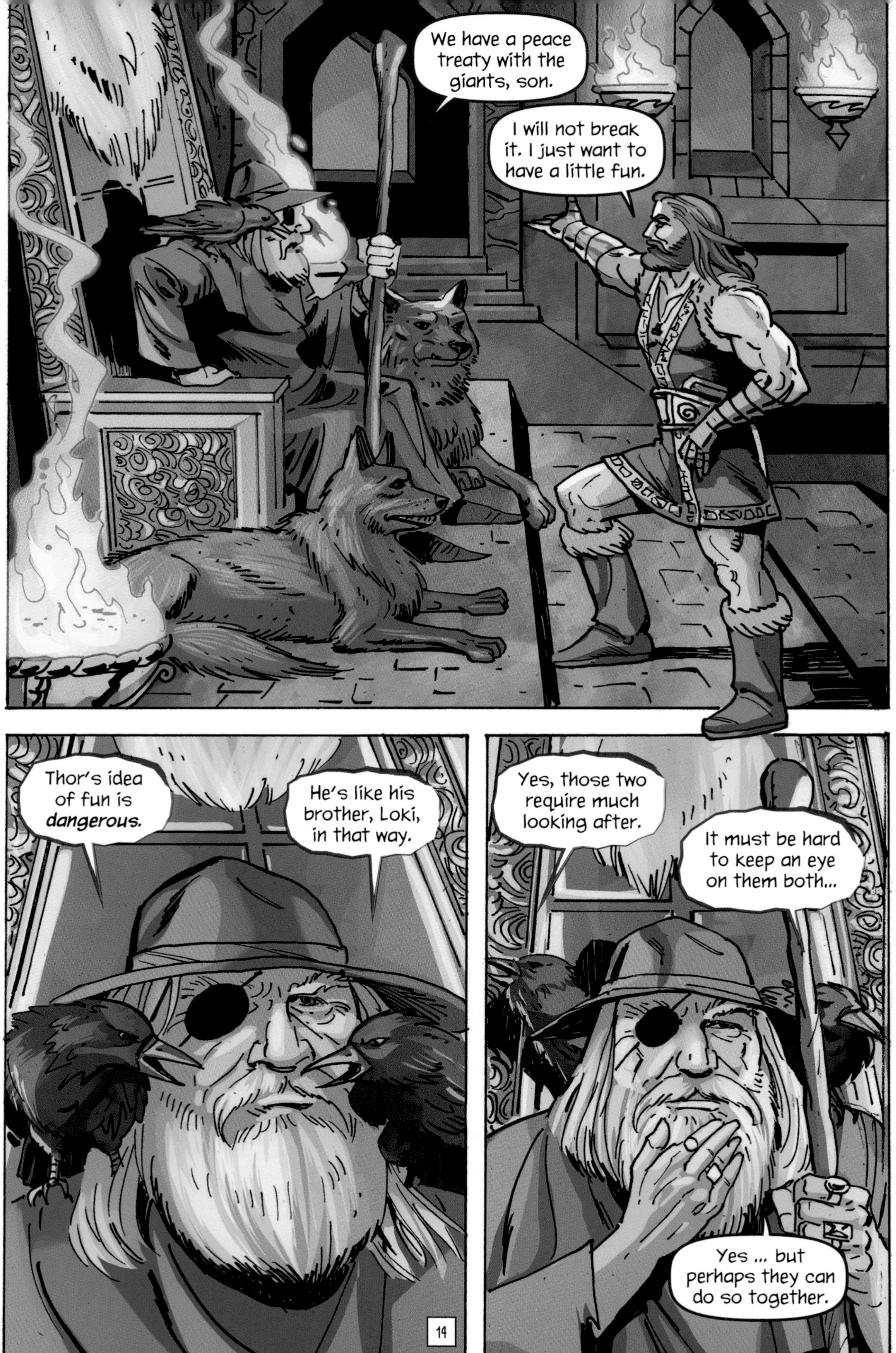
We have a peace treaty with the giants, son.
I will not break it. I just want to have a little fun.
Thor's idea of fun is *dangerous.*
He's like his brother, Loki, in that way.
Yes, those two require much looking after.
It must be hard to keep an eye on them both...
Yes ... but perhaps they can do so together.

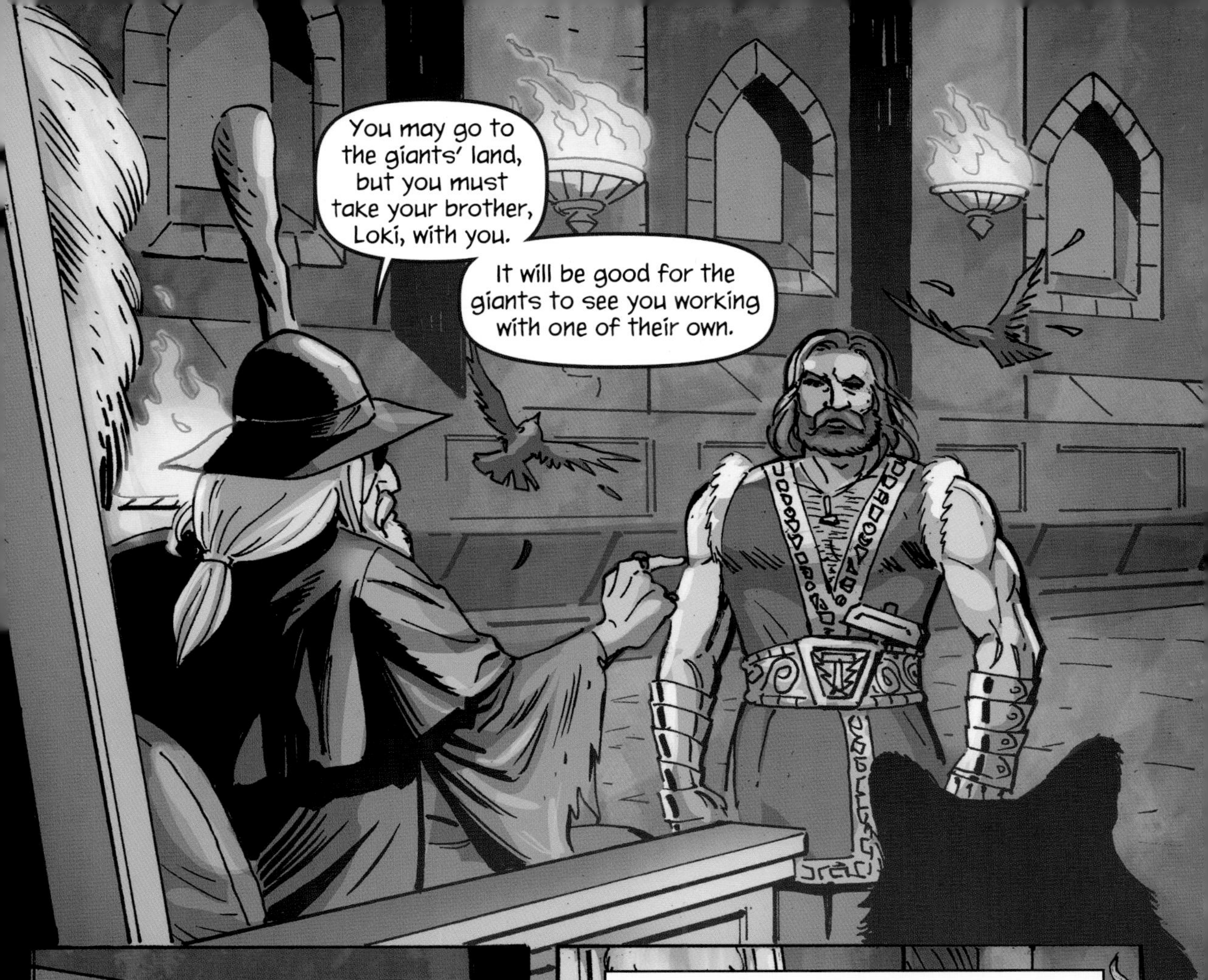
You may go to the giants' land, but you must take your brother, Loki, with you.
It will be good for the giants to see you working with one of their own.

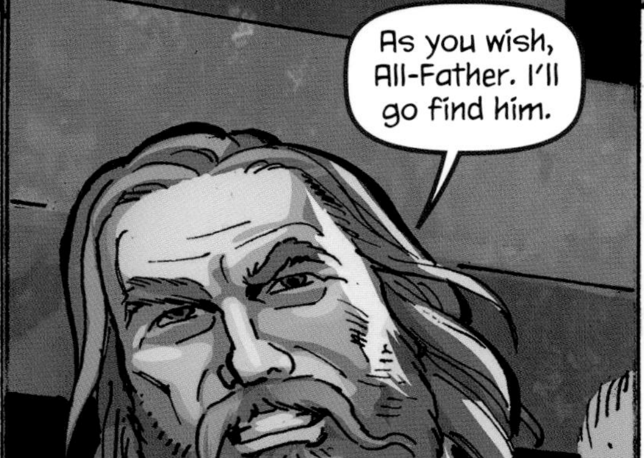
As you wish, All-Father. I'll go find him.

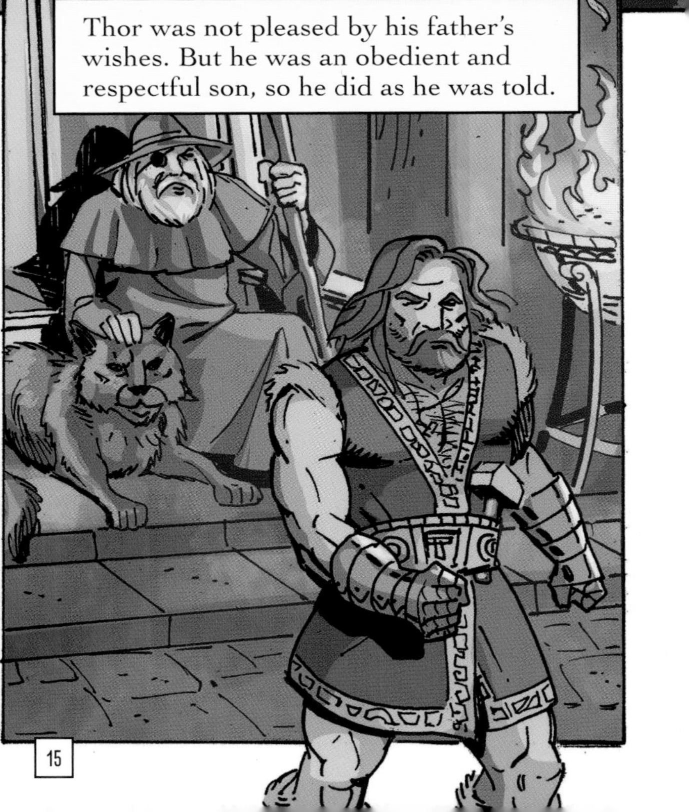
Thor was not pleased by his father's wishes. But he was an obedient and respectful son, so he did as he was told.

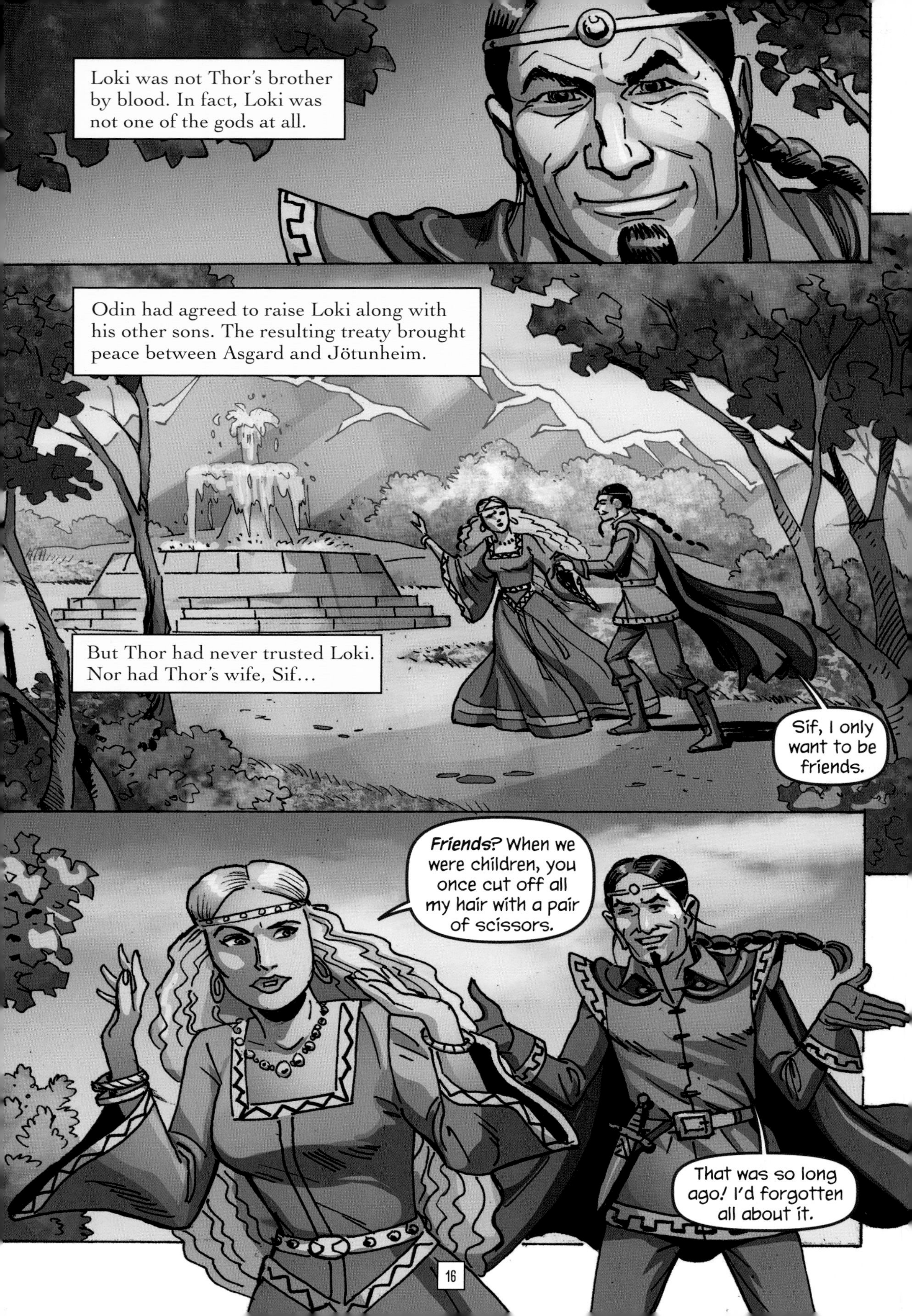

Loki was not Thor's brother by blood. In fact, Loki was not one of the gods at all.
Odin had agreed to raise Loki along with his other sons. The resulting treaty brought peace between Asgard and Jötunheim.
But Thor had never trusted Loki. Nor had Thor's wife, Sif…
Sif, I only want to be friends.
Friends? When we were children, you once cut off all my hair with a pair of scissors.
That was so long ago! I'd forgotten all about it.

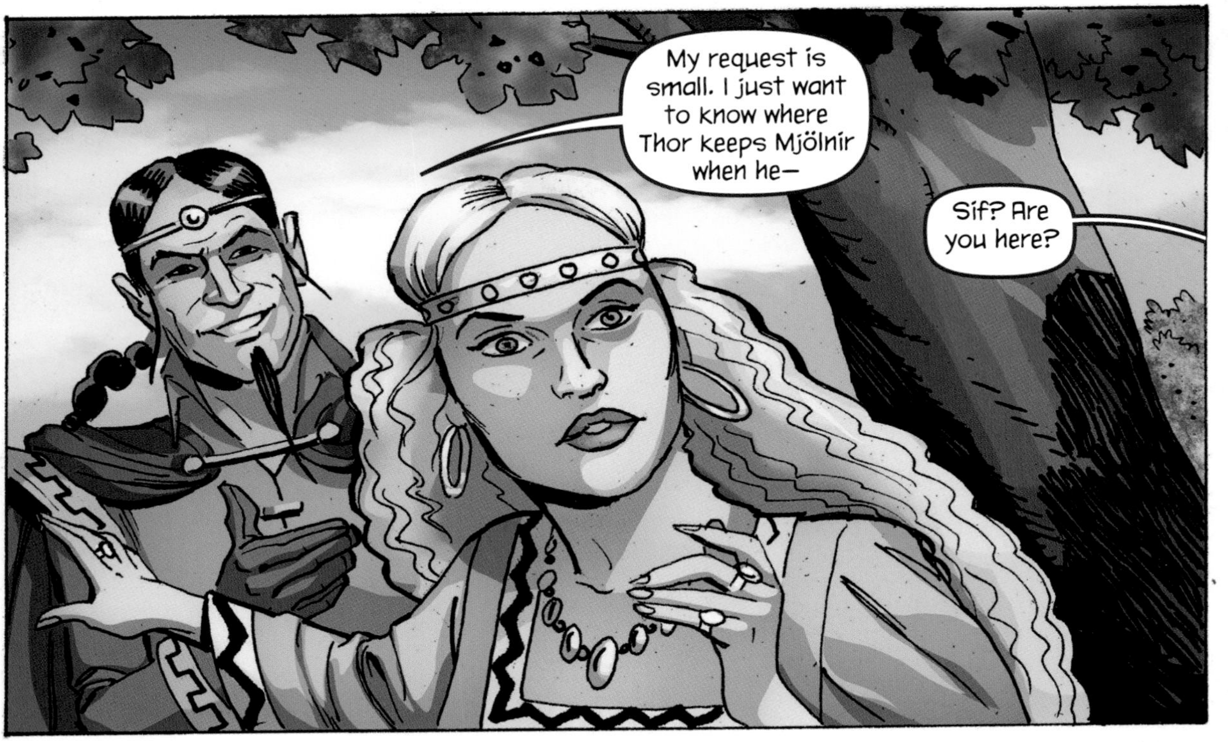
My request is small. I just want to know where Thor keeps Mjölnir when he—
Sif? Are you here?
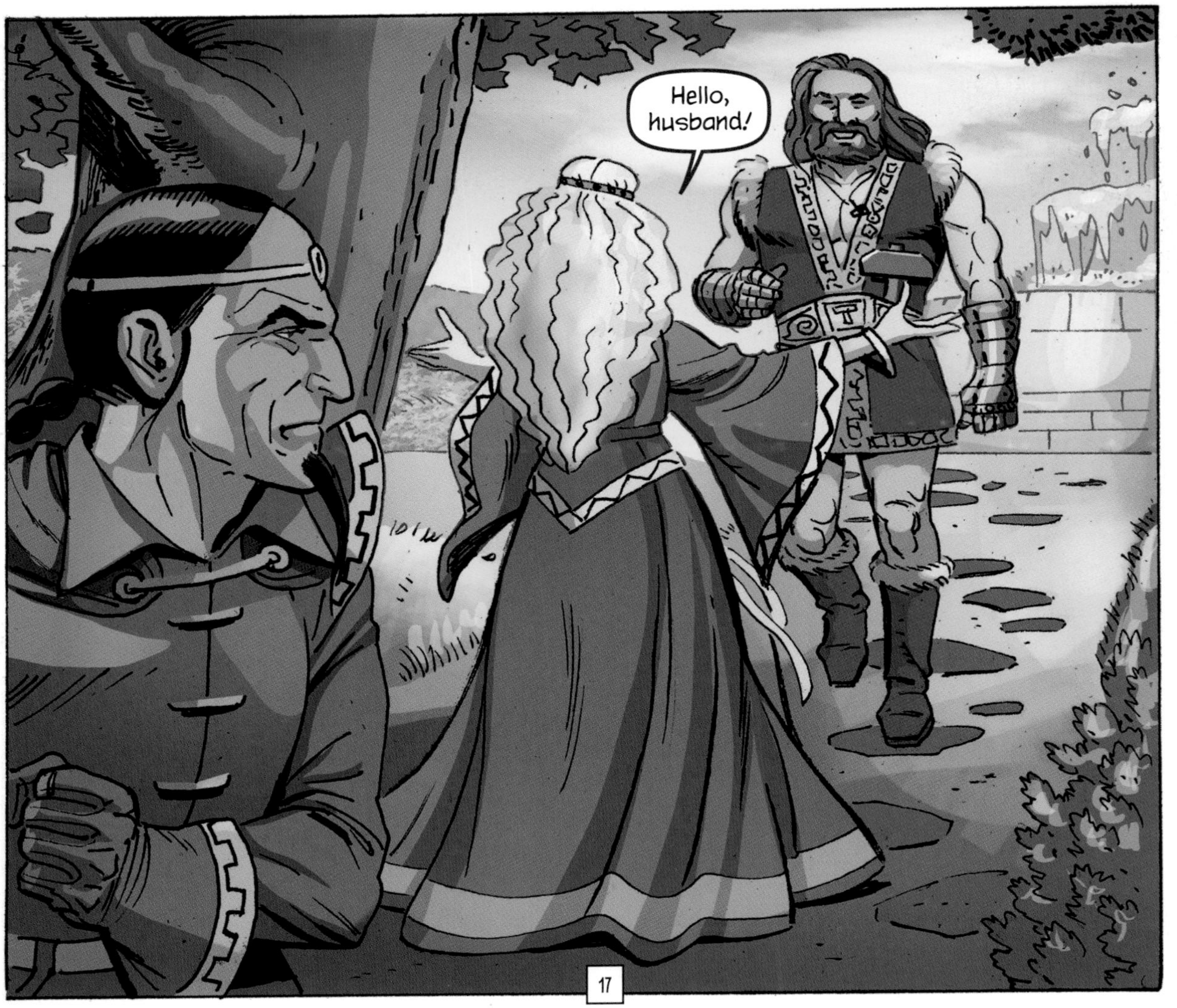
Hello, husband!

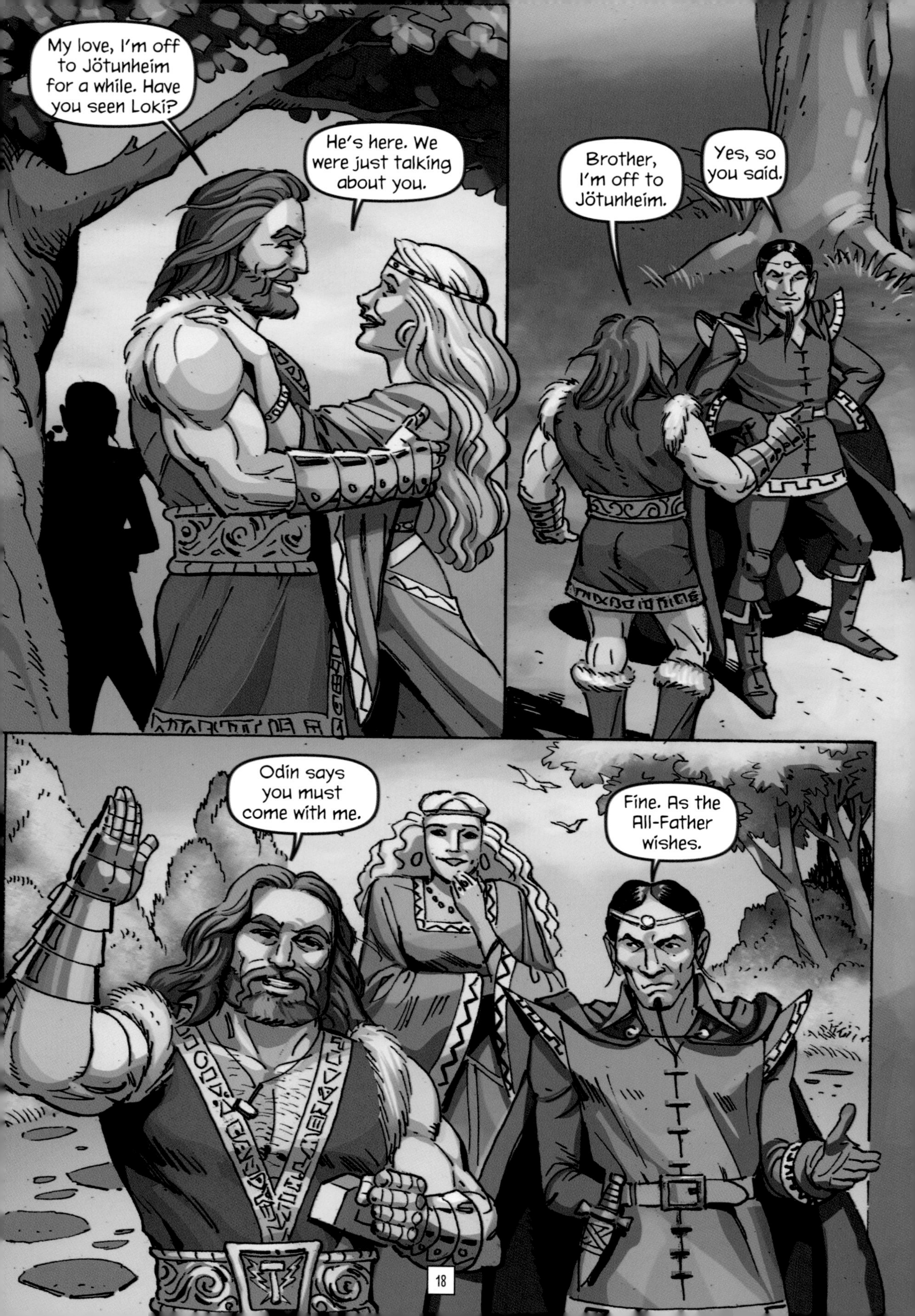
My love, I'm off to Jötunheim for a while. Have you seen Loki?
He's here. We were just talking about you.
Brother, I'm off to Jötunheim.
Yes, so you said.
Odin says you must come with me.
Fine. As the All-Father wishes.

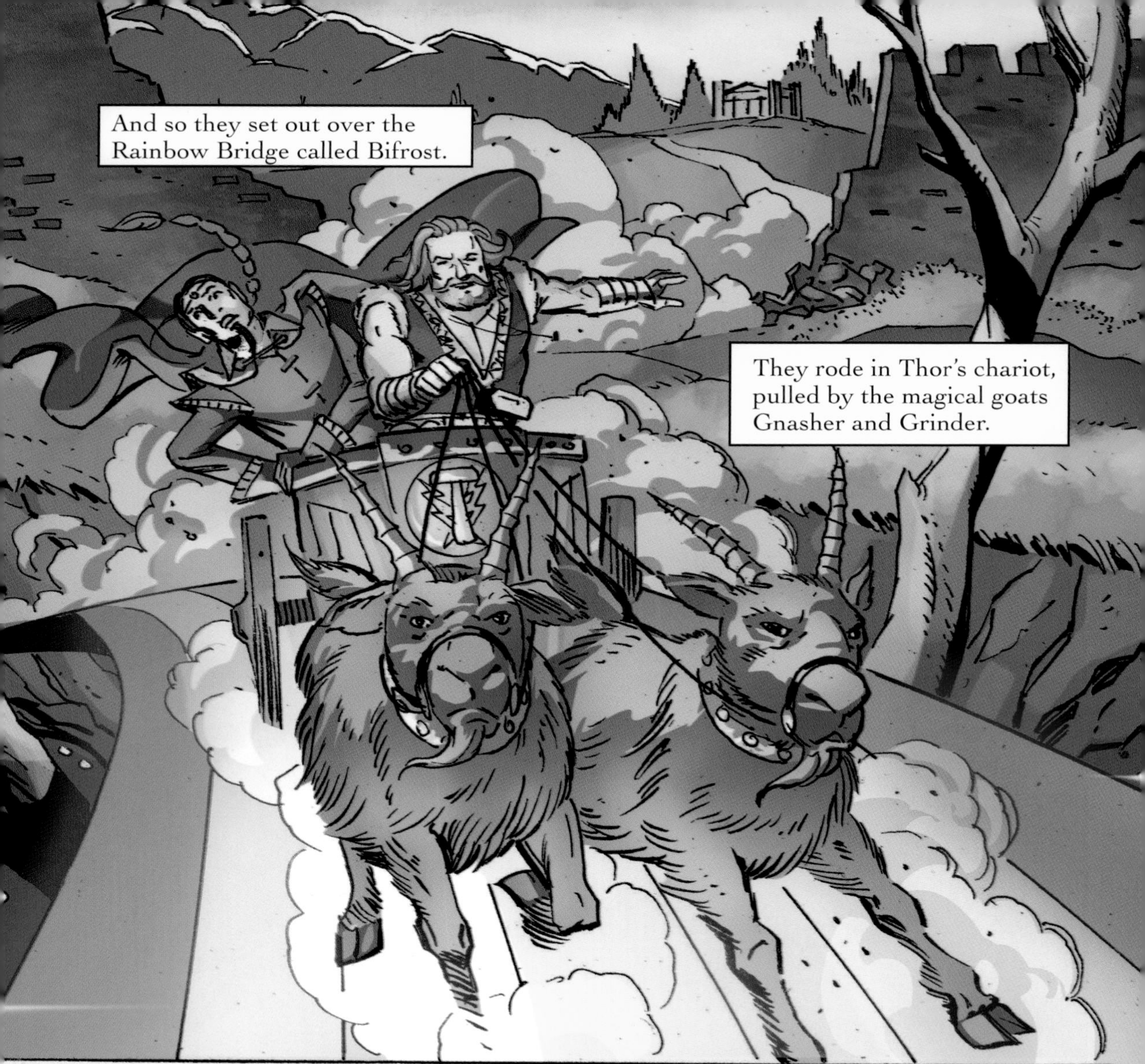
And so they set out over the Rainbow Bridge called Bifrost.
They rode in Thor's chariot, pulled by the magical goats Gnasher and Grinder.

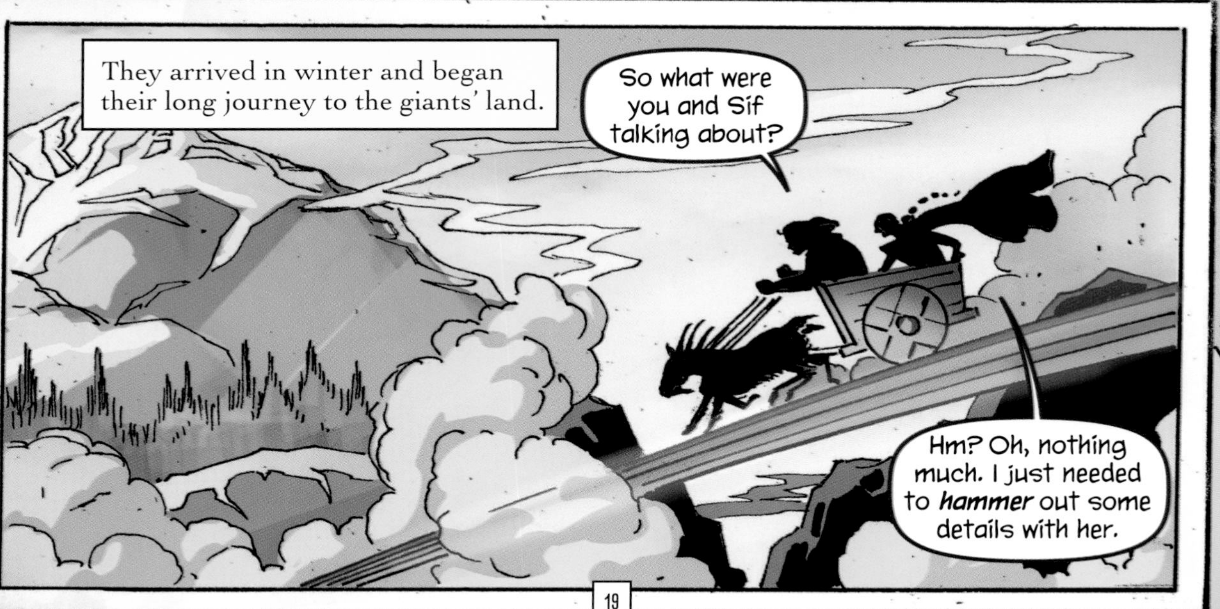
They arrived in winter and began their long journey to the giants' land.
So what were you and Sif talking about?
Hm? Oh, nothing much. I just needed to hammer out some details with her.

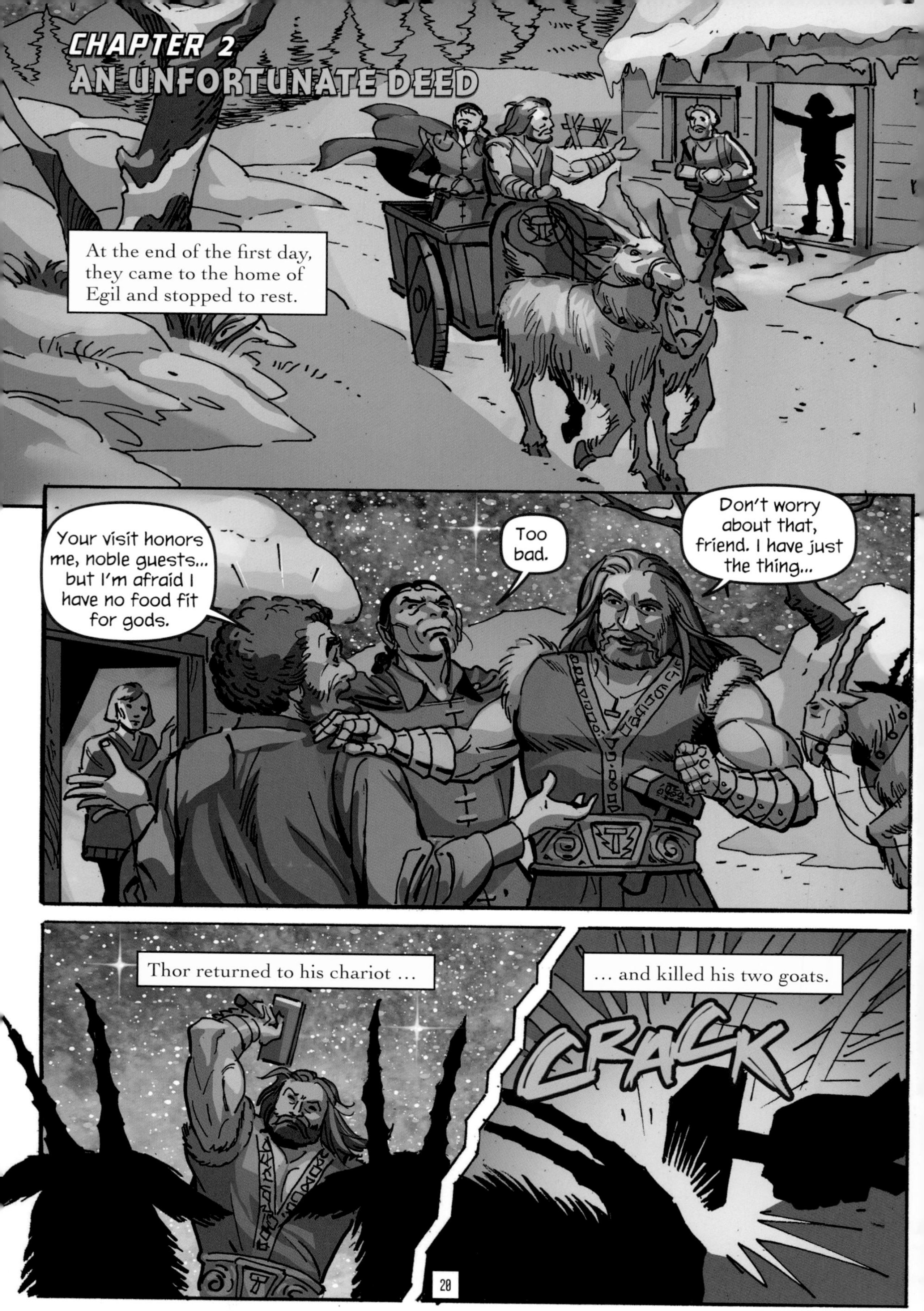
CHAPTER 2
AN UNFORTUNATE DEED
At the end of the first day, they came to the home of Egil and stopped to rest.
Your visit honors me, noble guests... but I'm afraid I have no food fit for gods.
Too bad.
Don't worry about that, friend. I have just the thing...
Thor returned to his chariot ...
... and killed his two goats.
CRACK

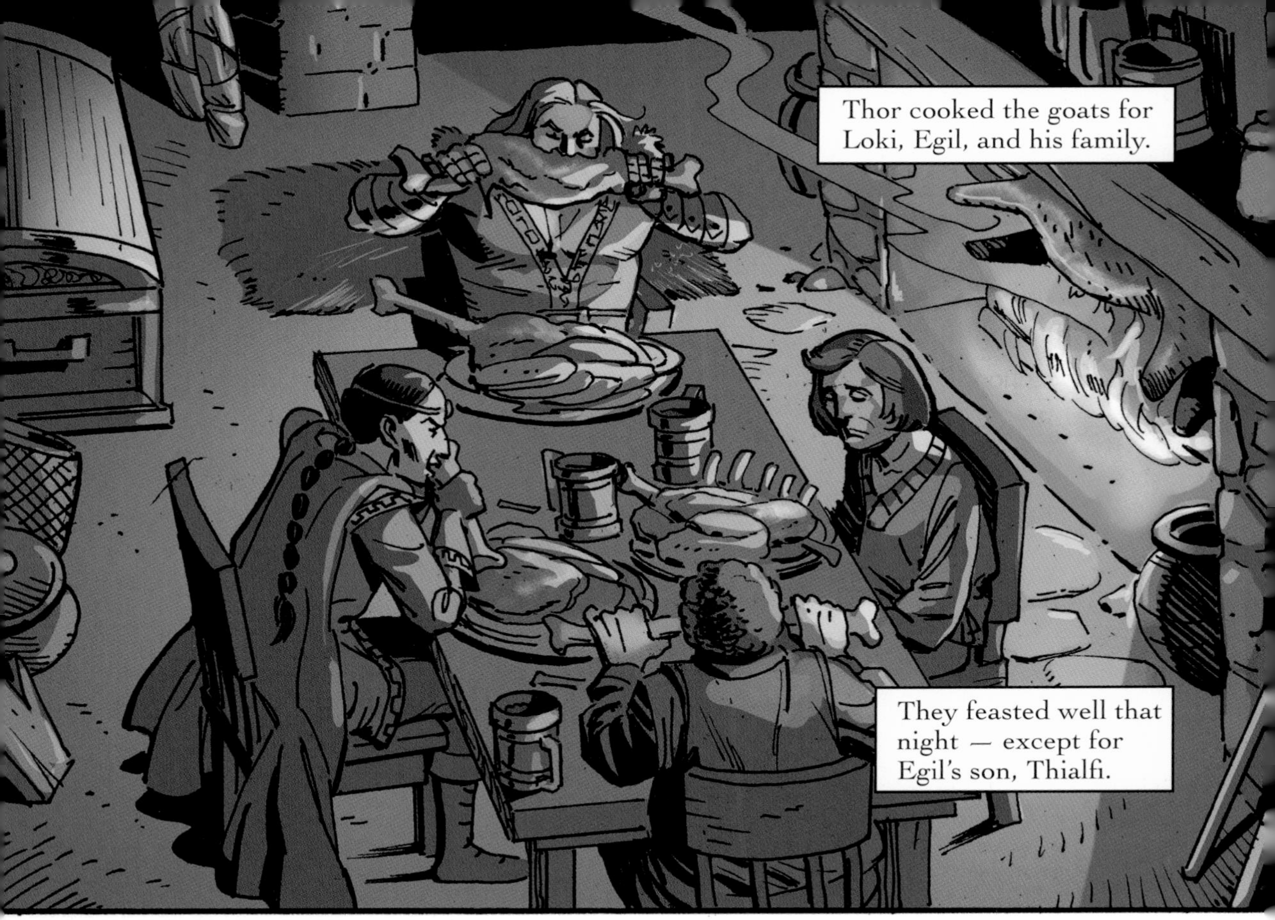
Thor cooked the goats for Loki, Egil, and his family.
They feasted well that night — except for Egil's son, Thialfi.

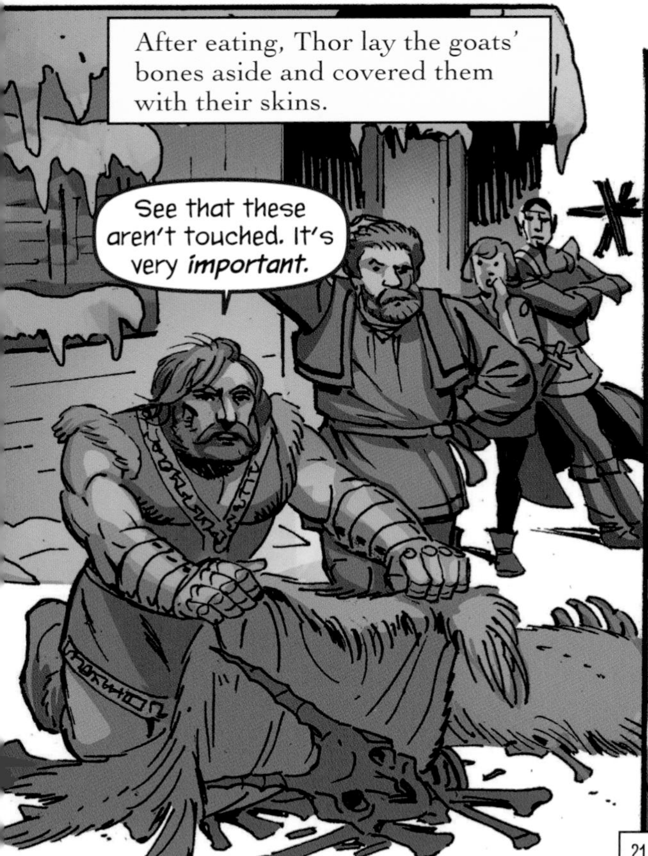
After eating, Thor lay the goats' bones aside and covered them with their skins.
See that these aren't touched. It's very *important*.

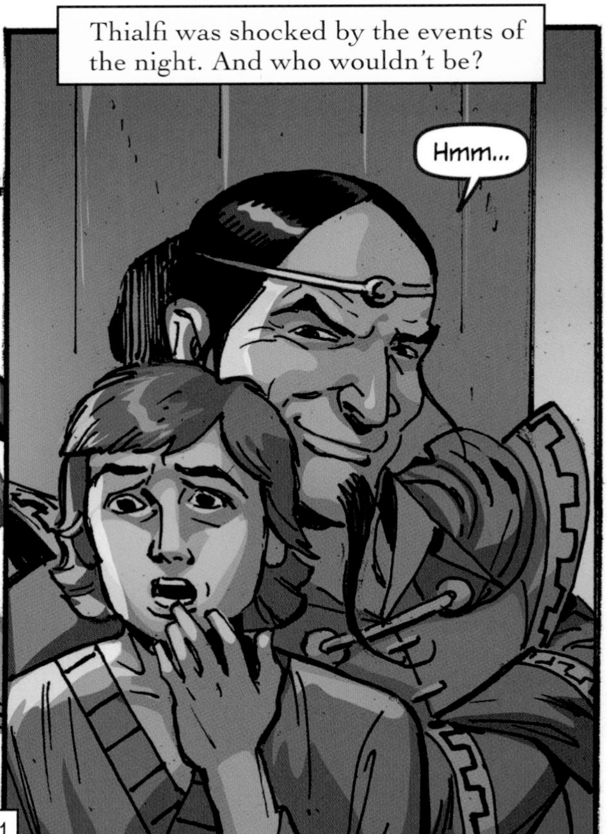
Thialfi was shocked by the events of the night. And who wouldn't be?
Hmm...

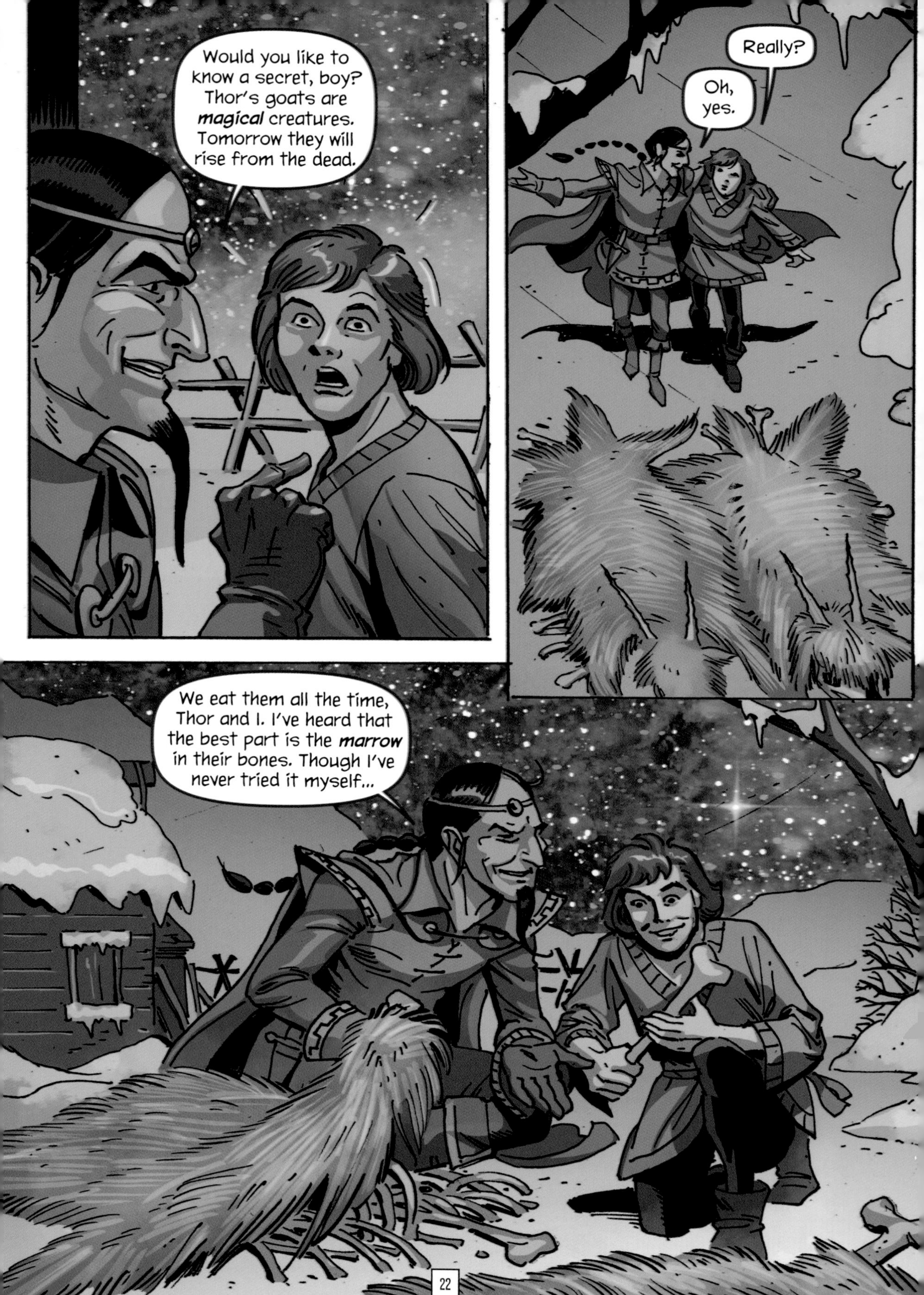
Would you like to know a secret, boy? Thor's goats are *magical* creatures. Tomorrow they will rise from the dead.
Really?
Oh, yes.
We eat them all the time, Thor and I. I've heard that the best part is the *marrow* in their bones. Though I've never tried it myself...

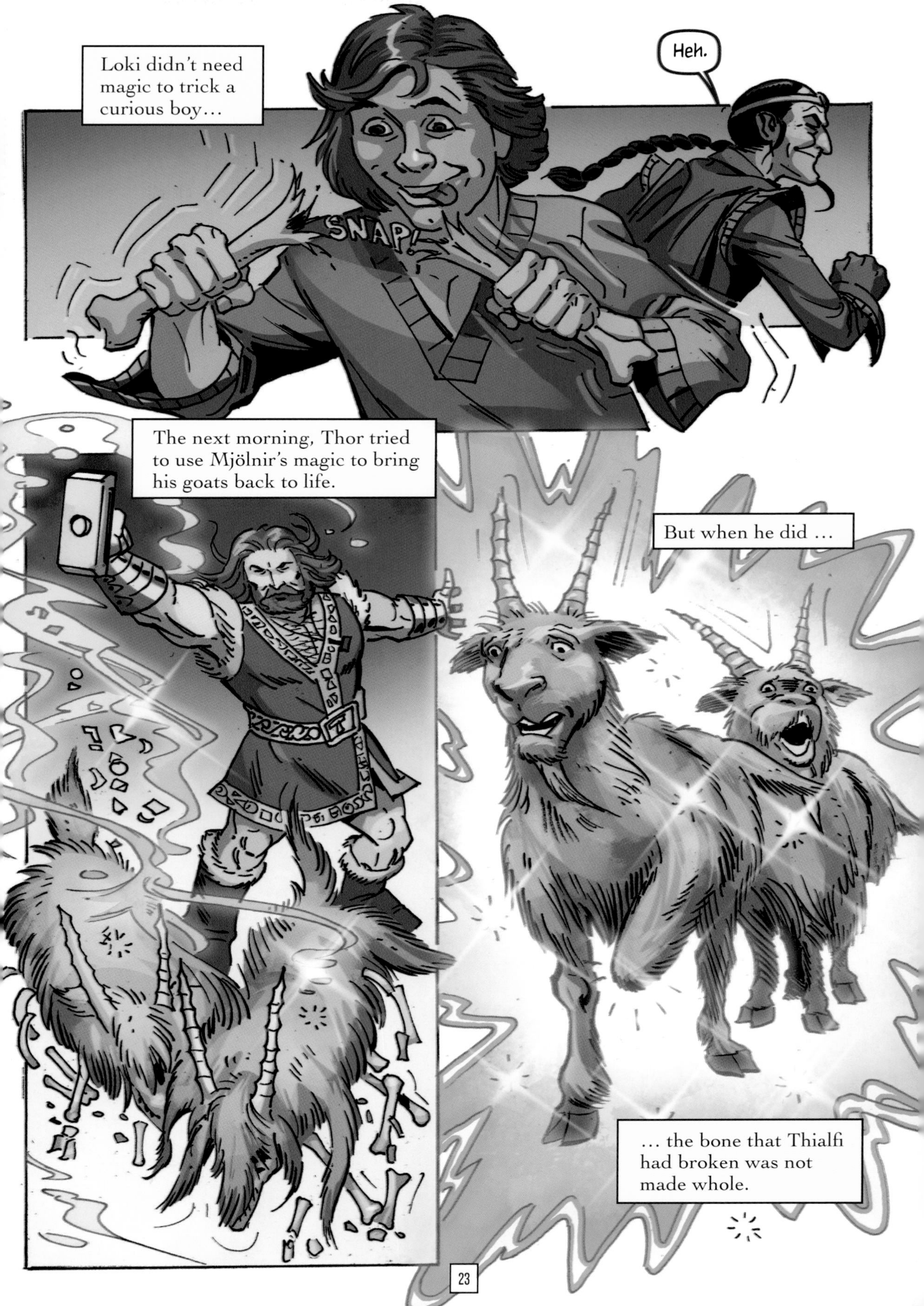
Loki didn't need magic to trick a curious boy...
Heh.
SNAP!
The next morning, Thor tried to use Mjölnir's magic to bring his goats back to life.
But when he did ...
... the bone that Thialfi had broken was not made whole.

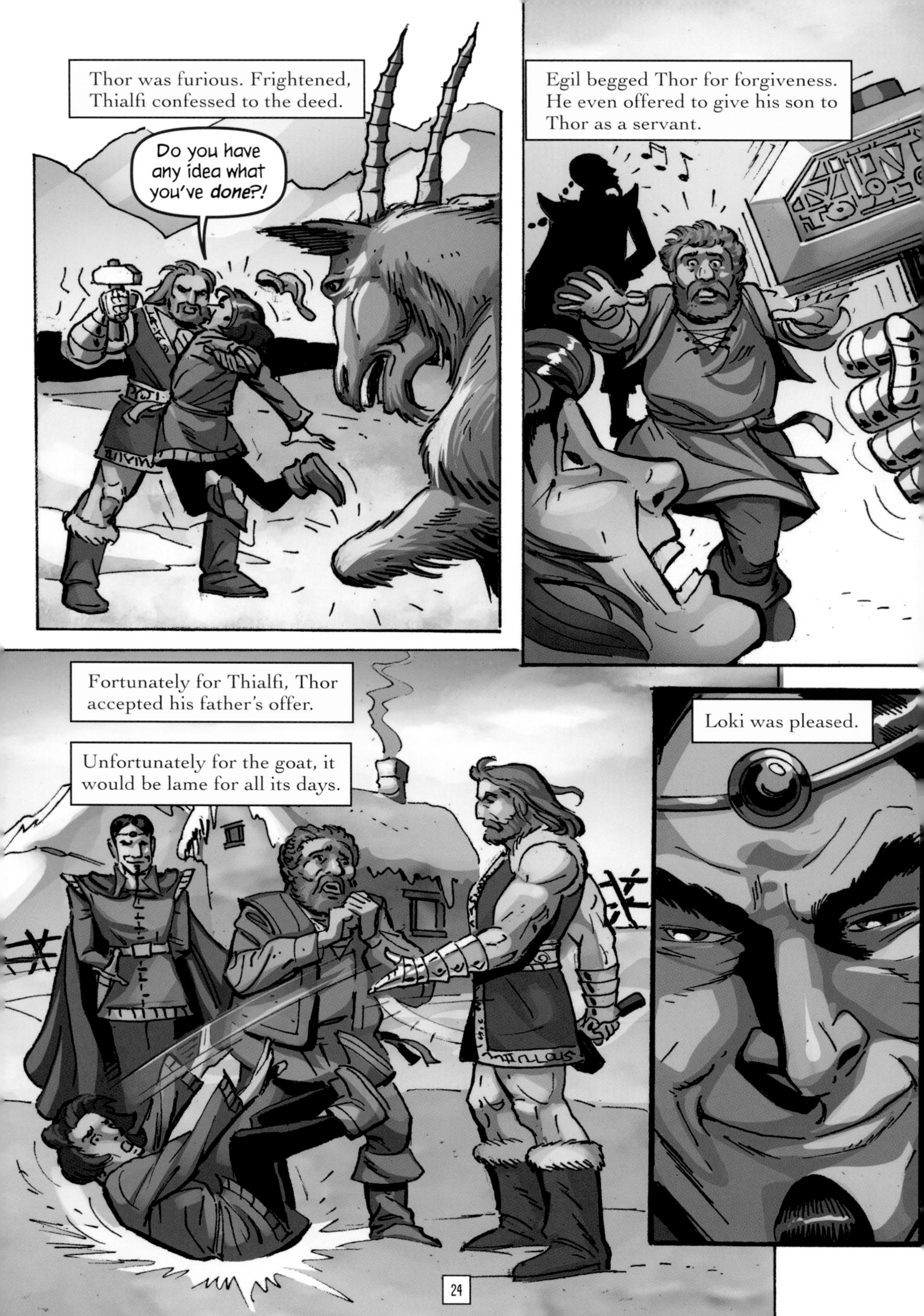
Thor was furious. Frightened, Thialfi confessed to the deed.
Do you have any idea what you've ***done***?!
Egil begged Thor for forgiveness. He even offered to give his son to Thor as a servant.
Fortunately for Thialfi, Thor accepted his father's offer.
Unfortunately for the goat, it would be lame for all its days.
Loki was pleased.

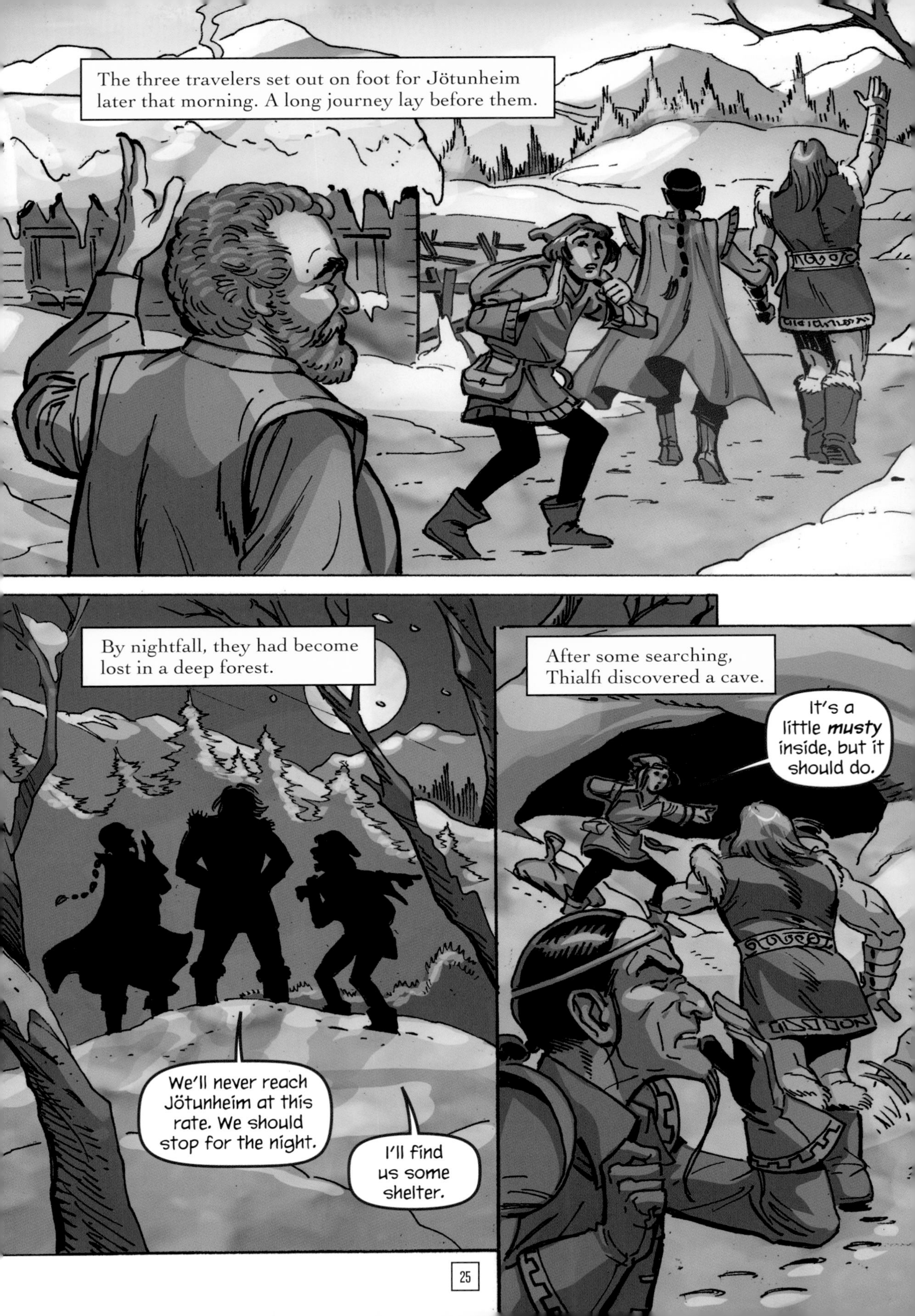
The three travelers set out on foot for Jötunheim later that morning. A long journey lay before them.
By nightfall, they had become lost in a deep forest.
We'll never reach Jötunheim at this rate. We should stop for the night.
I'll find us some shelter.
After some searching, Thialfi discovered a cave.
It's a little ***musty*** inside, but it should do.

CHAPTER 3
A GIANT AWAKENS

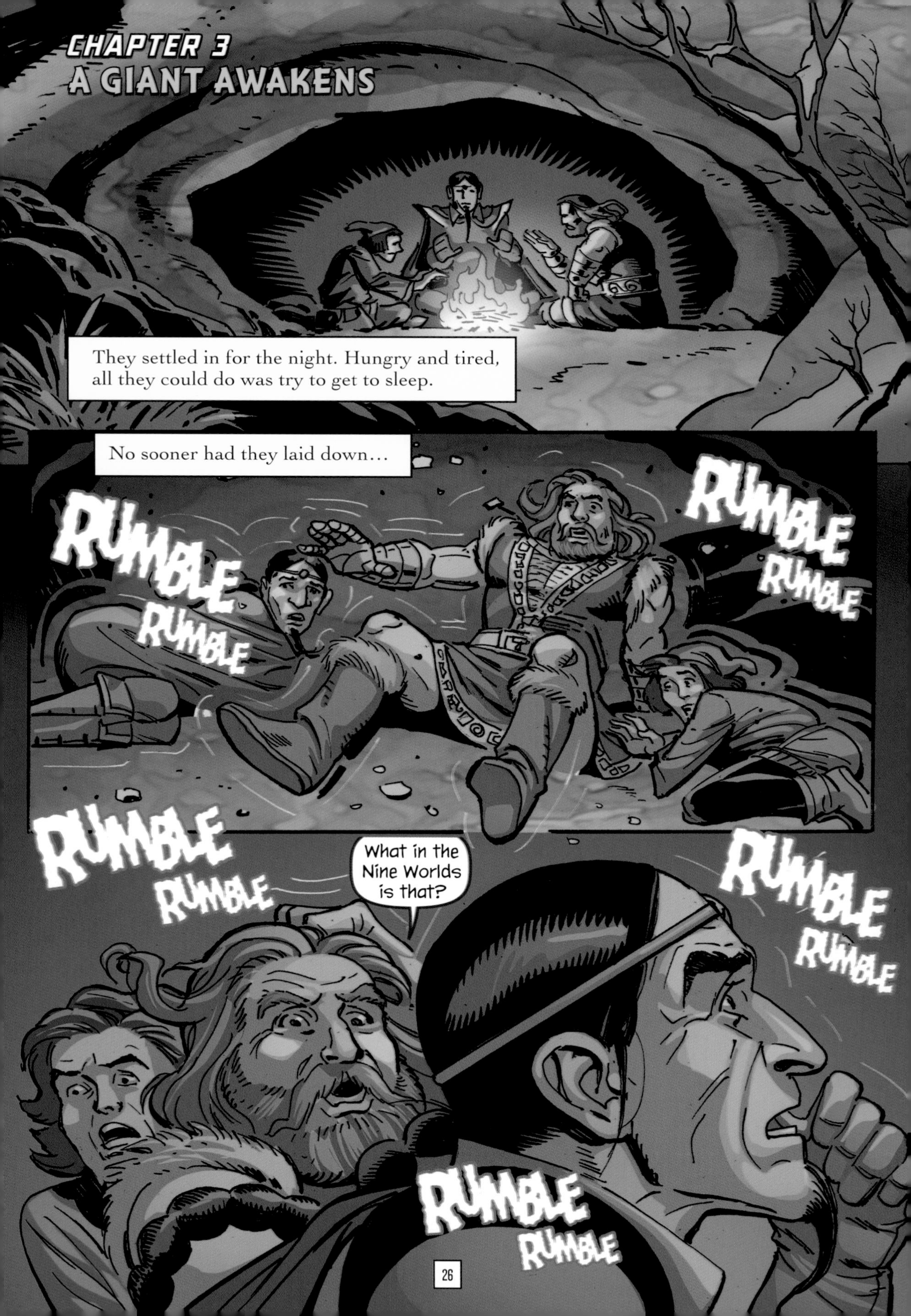
They settled in for the night. Hungry and tired, all they could do was try to get to sleep.
No sooner had they laid down…
RUMBLE RUMBLE
RUMBLE RUMBLE
RUMBLE RUMBLE
What in the Nine Worlds is that?
RUMBLE RUMBLE
RUMBLE RUMBLE

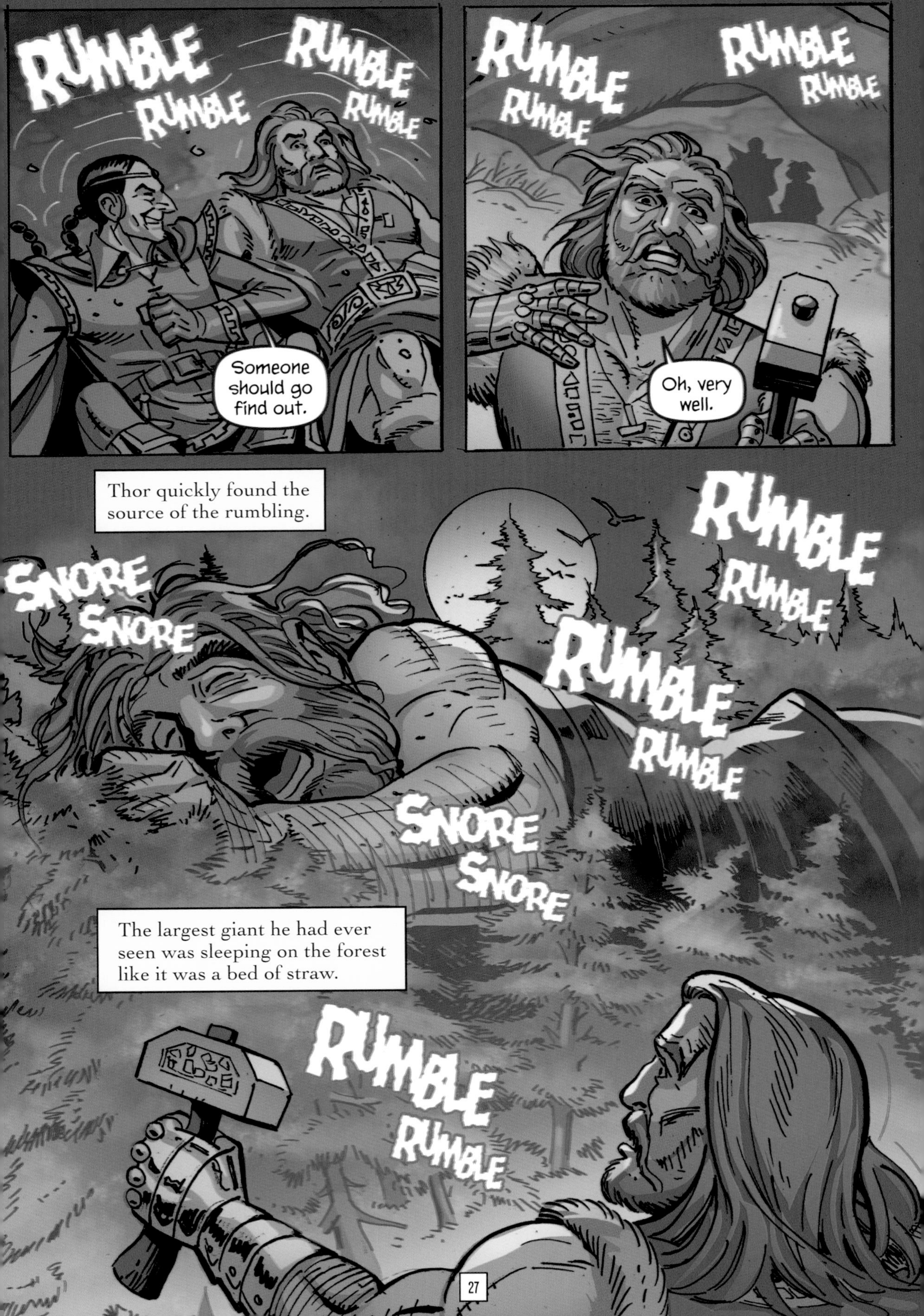
RUMBLE
RUMBLE
RUMBLE
RUMBLE
Someone should go find out.
RUMBLE
RUMBLE
RUMBLE
RUMBLE
Oh, very well.
Thor quickly found the source of the rumbling.
SNORE
SNORE
RUMBLE
RUMBLE
RUMBLE
RUMBLE
SNORE
SNORE
The largest giant he had ever seen was sleeping on the forest like it was a bed of straw.
RUMBLE
RUMBLE

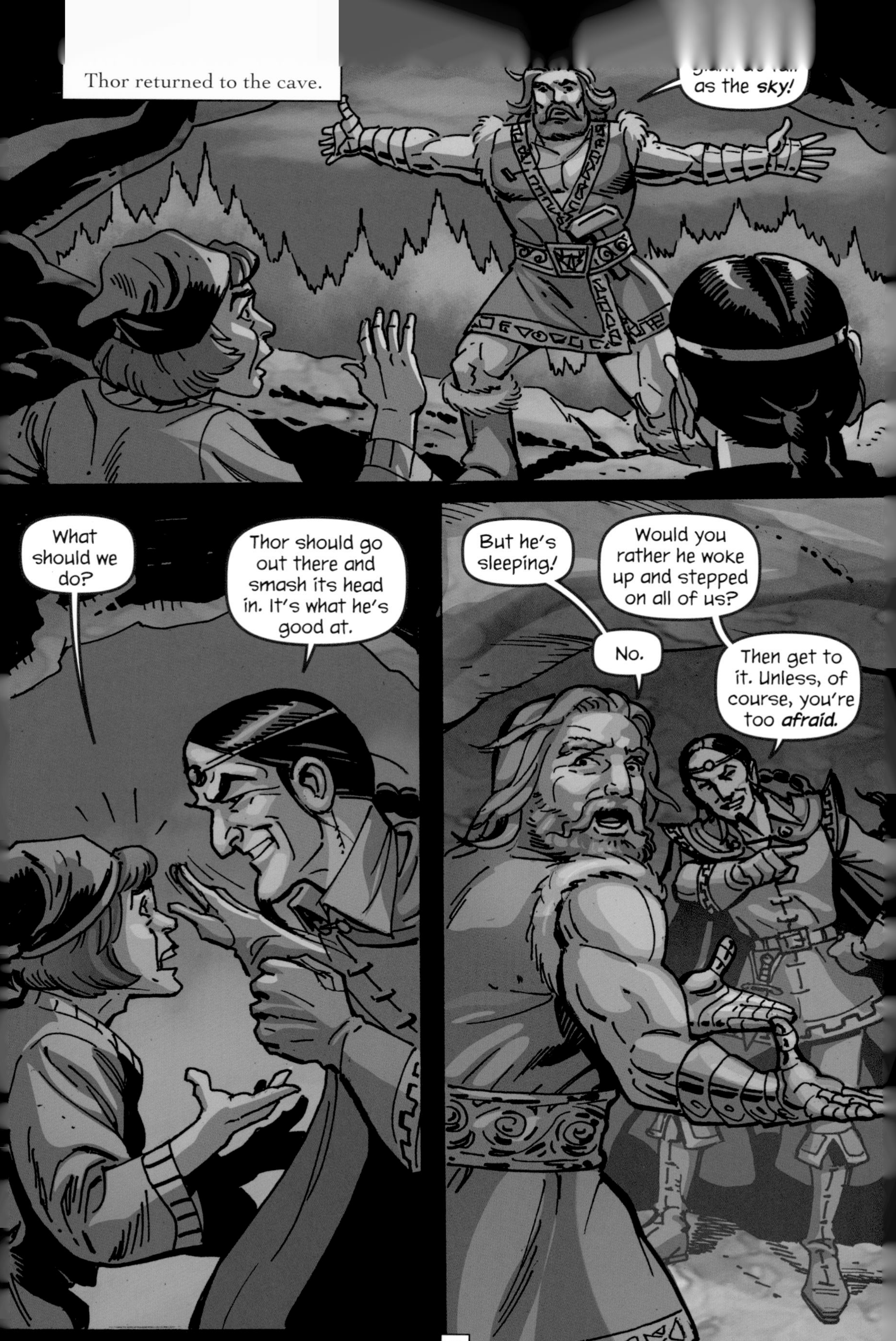
Thor returned to the cave.
as the sky!
What should we do?
Thor should go out there and smash its head in. It's what he's good at.
But he's sleeping!
Would you rather he woke up and stepped on all of us?
No.
Then get to it. Unless, of course, you're too *afraid.*

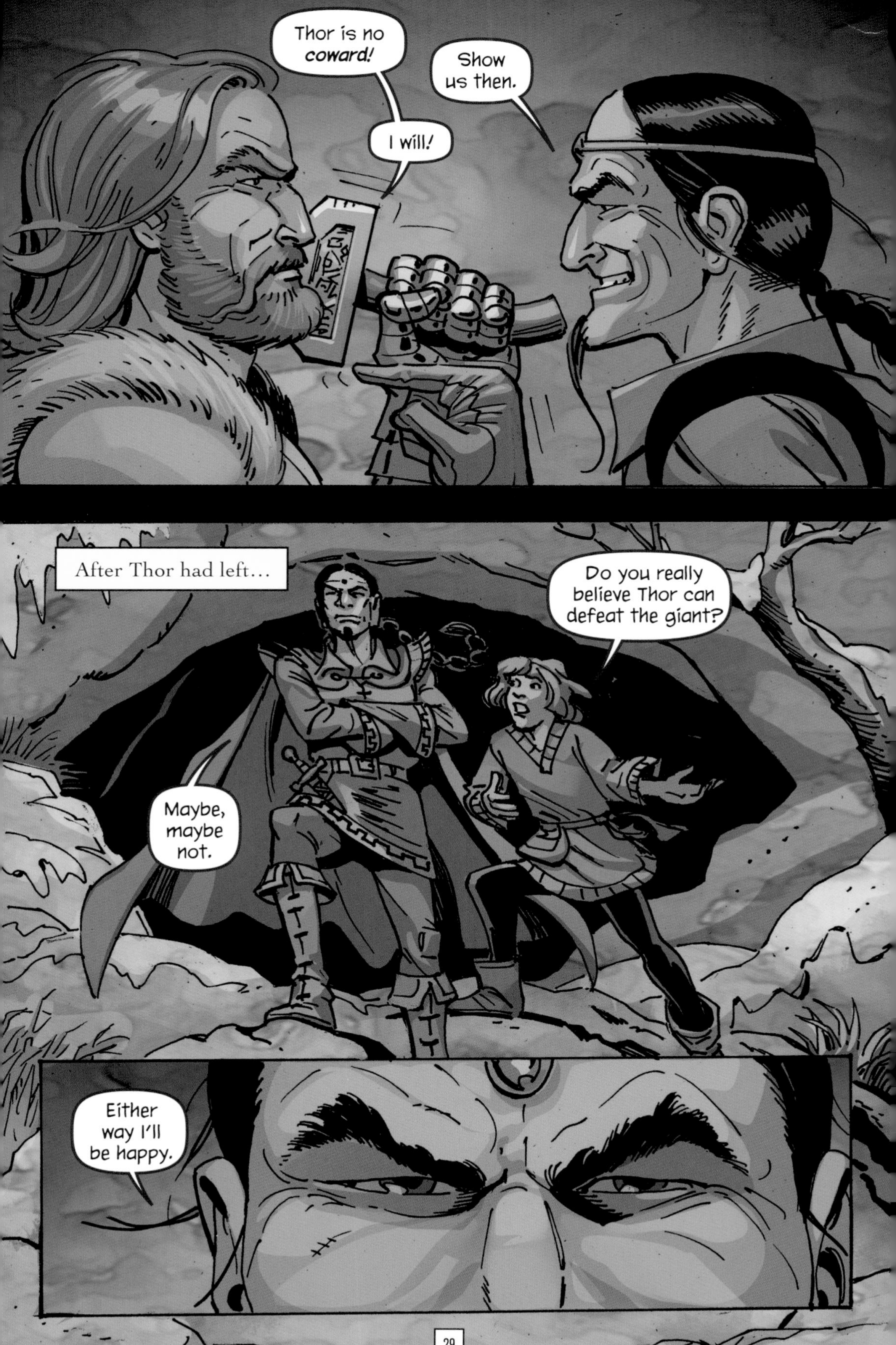
Thor is no *coward!*
I will!
Show us then.
After Thor had left...
Do you really believe Thor can defeat the giant?
Maybe, maybe not.
Either way I'll be happy.

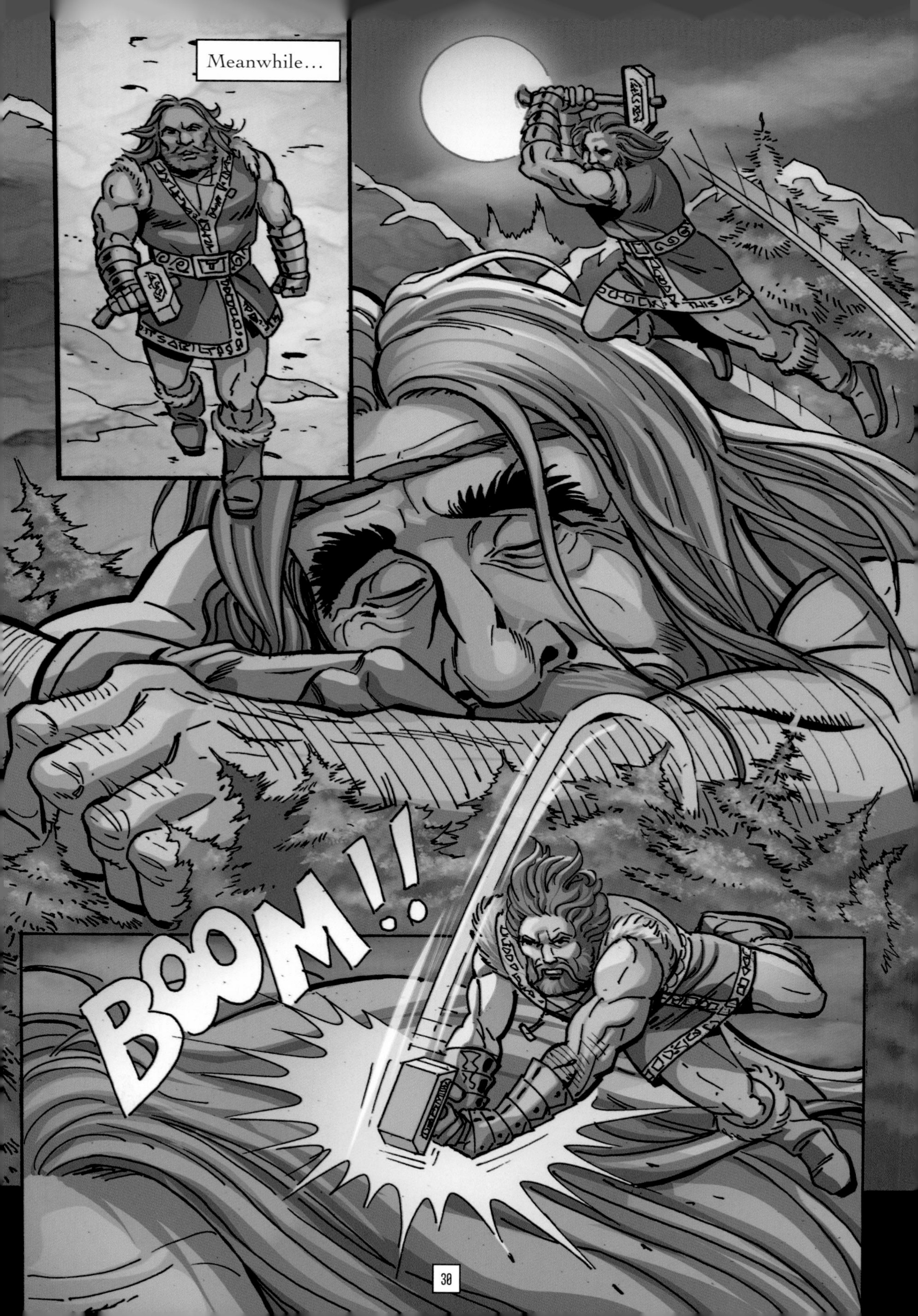
Meanwhile...
BOOM!!

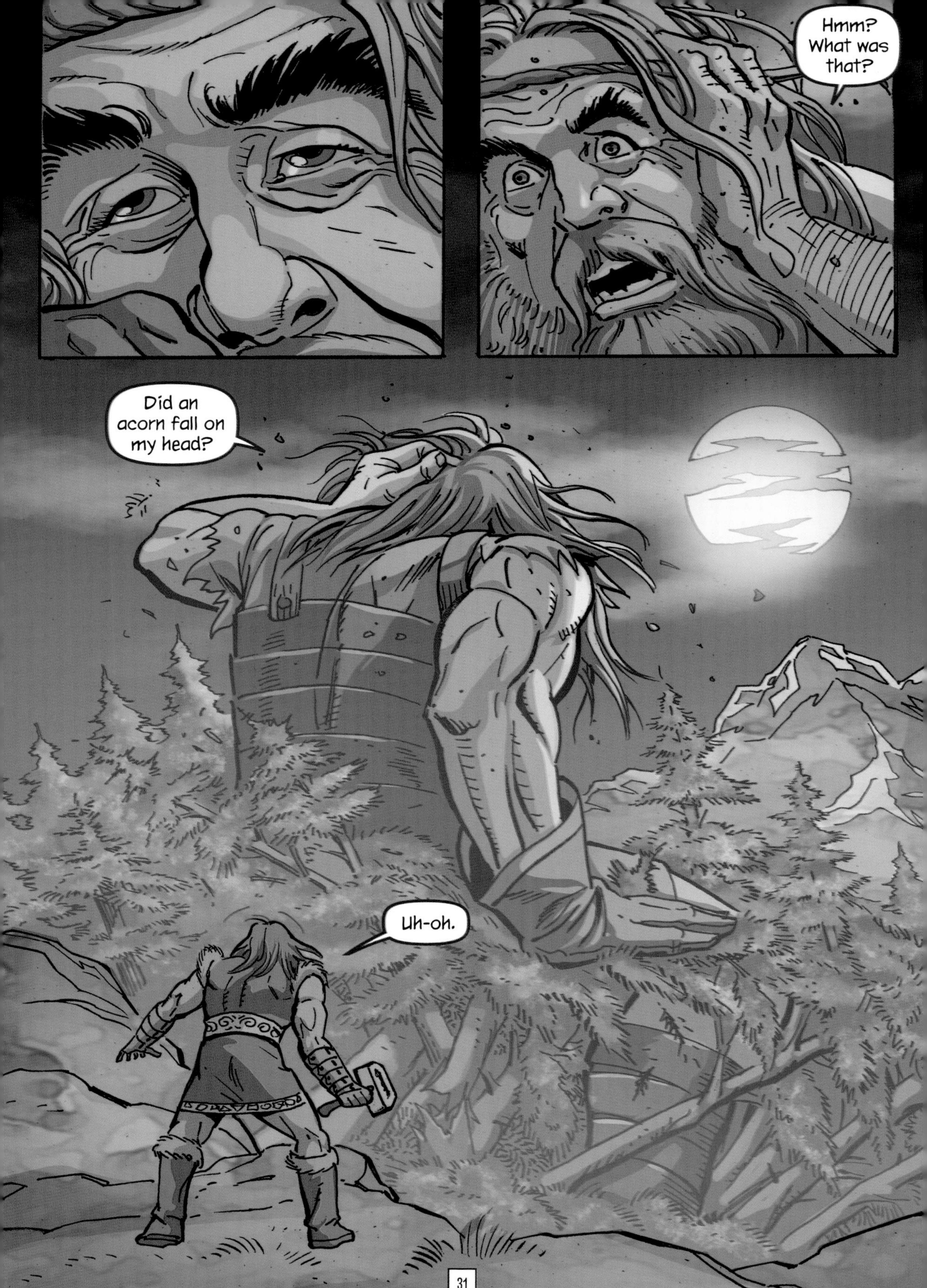
Hmm? What was that?
Did an acorn fall on my head?
Uh-oh.

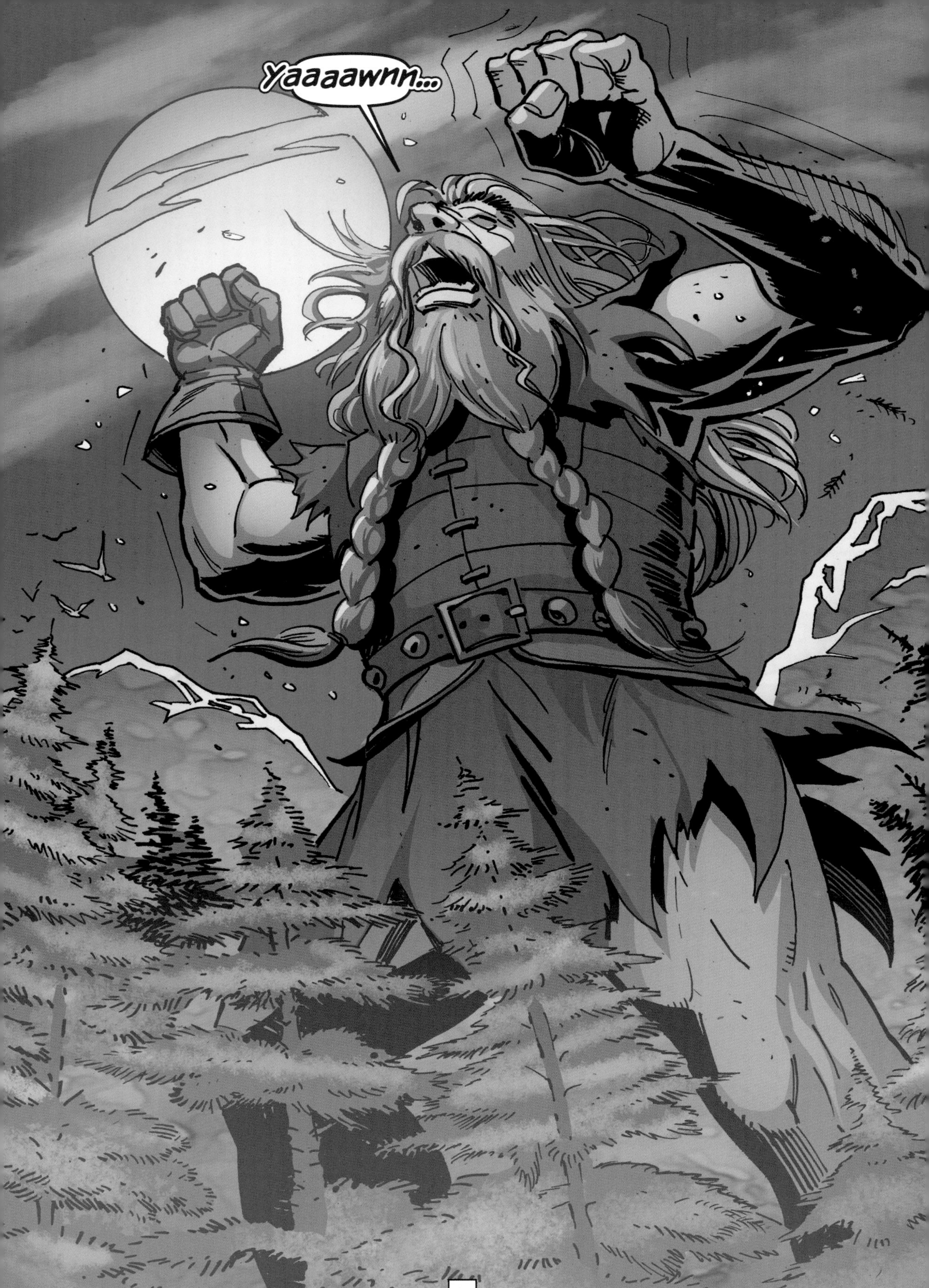
Yaaaawnn...

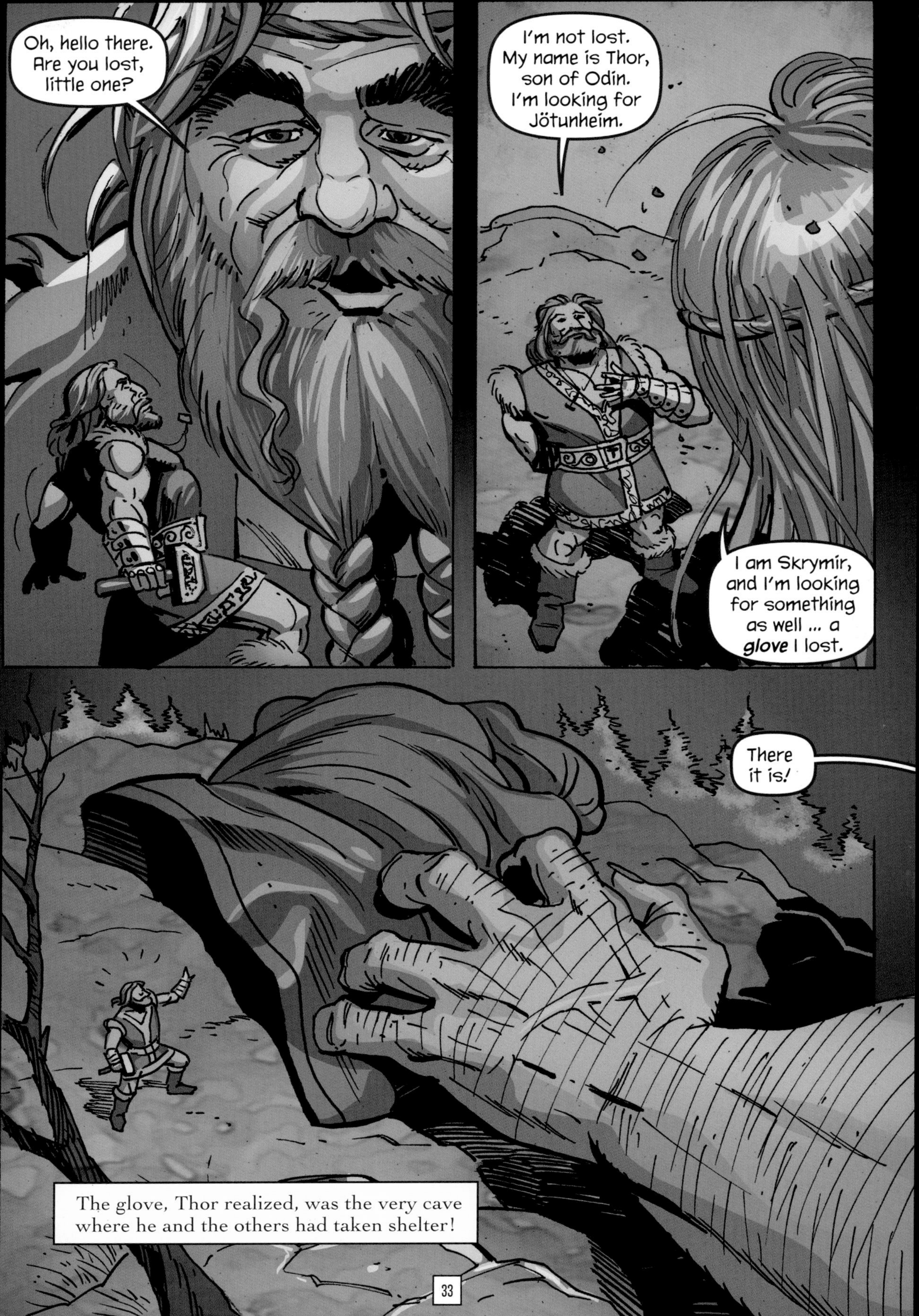
Oh, hello there. Are you lost, little one?
I'm not lost. My name is Thor, son of Odin. I'm looking for Jötunheim.
I am Skrymir, and I'm looking for something as well ... a *glove* I lost.
There it is!
The glove, Thor realized, was the very cave where he and the others had taken shelter!

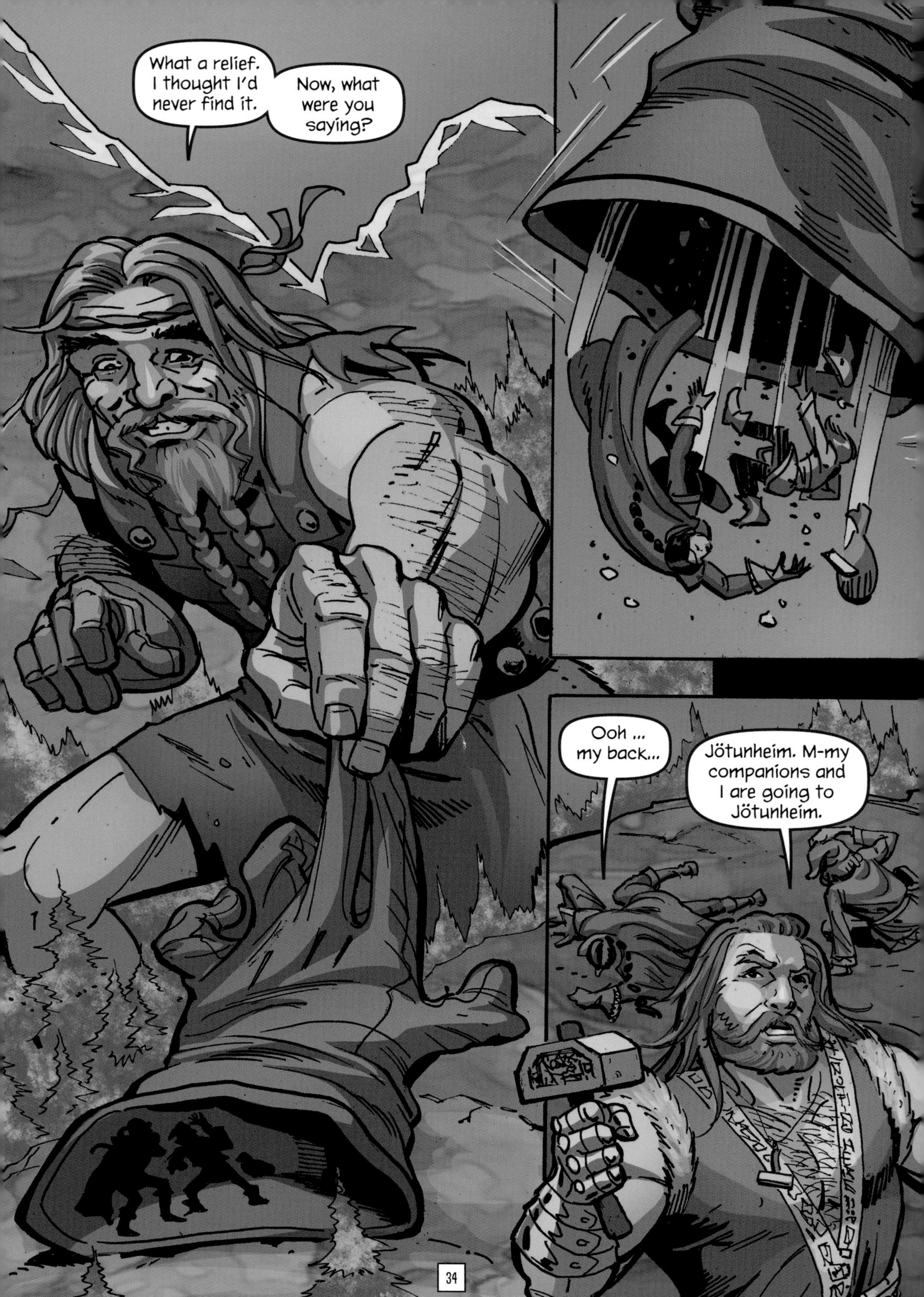

What a relief. I thought I'd never find it.
Now, what were you saying?
Ooh ... my back...
Jötunheim. M-my companions and I are going to Jötunheim.

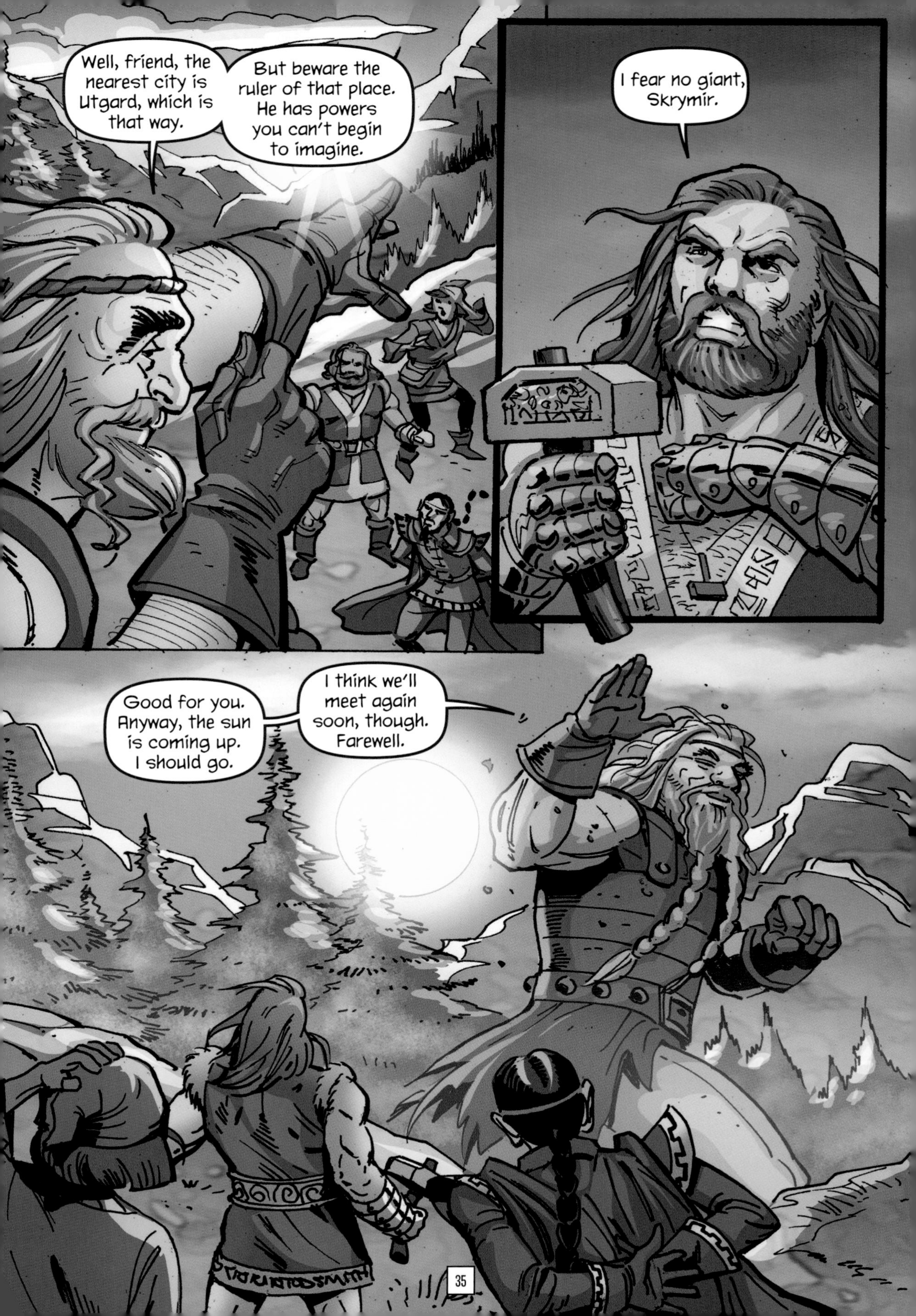
Well, friend, the nearest city is Utgard, which is that way.
But beware the ruler of that place. He has powers you can't begin to imagine.
I fear no giant, Skrymir.
Good for you. Anyway, the sun is coming up. I should go.
I think we'll meet again soon, though. Farewell.

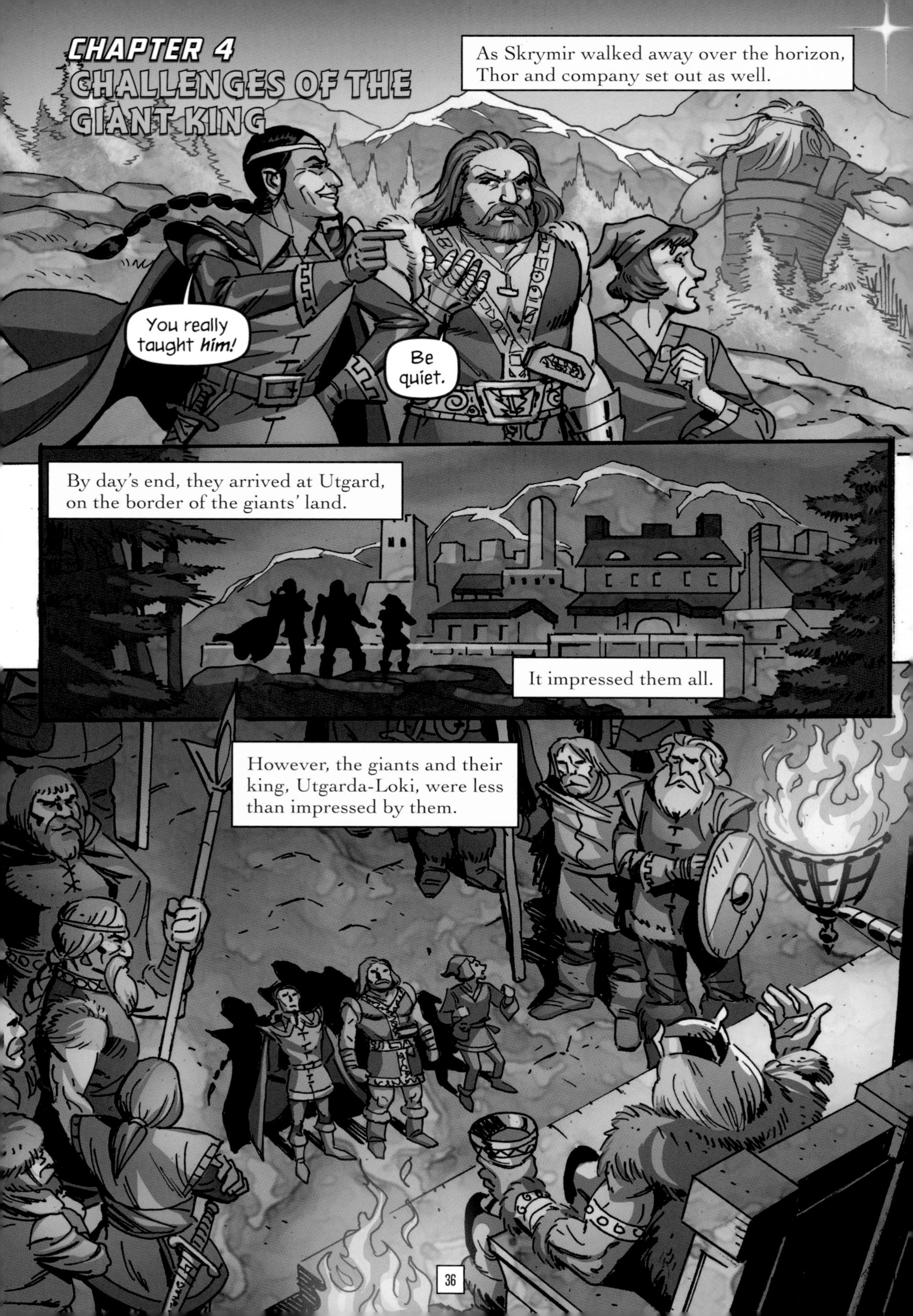
CHAPTER 4
CHALLENGES OF THE GIANT KING
As Skrymir walked away over the horizon, Thor and company set out as well.
You really taught *him!*
Be quiet.
By day's end, they arrived at Utgard, on the border of the giants' land.
It impressed them all.
However, the giants and their king, Utgarda-Loki, were less than impressed by them.

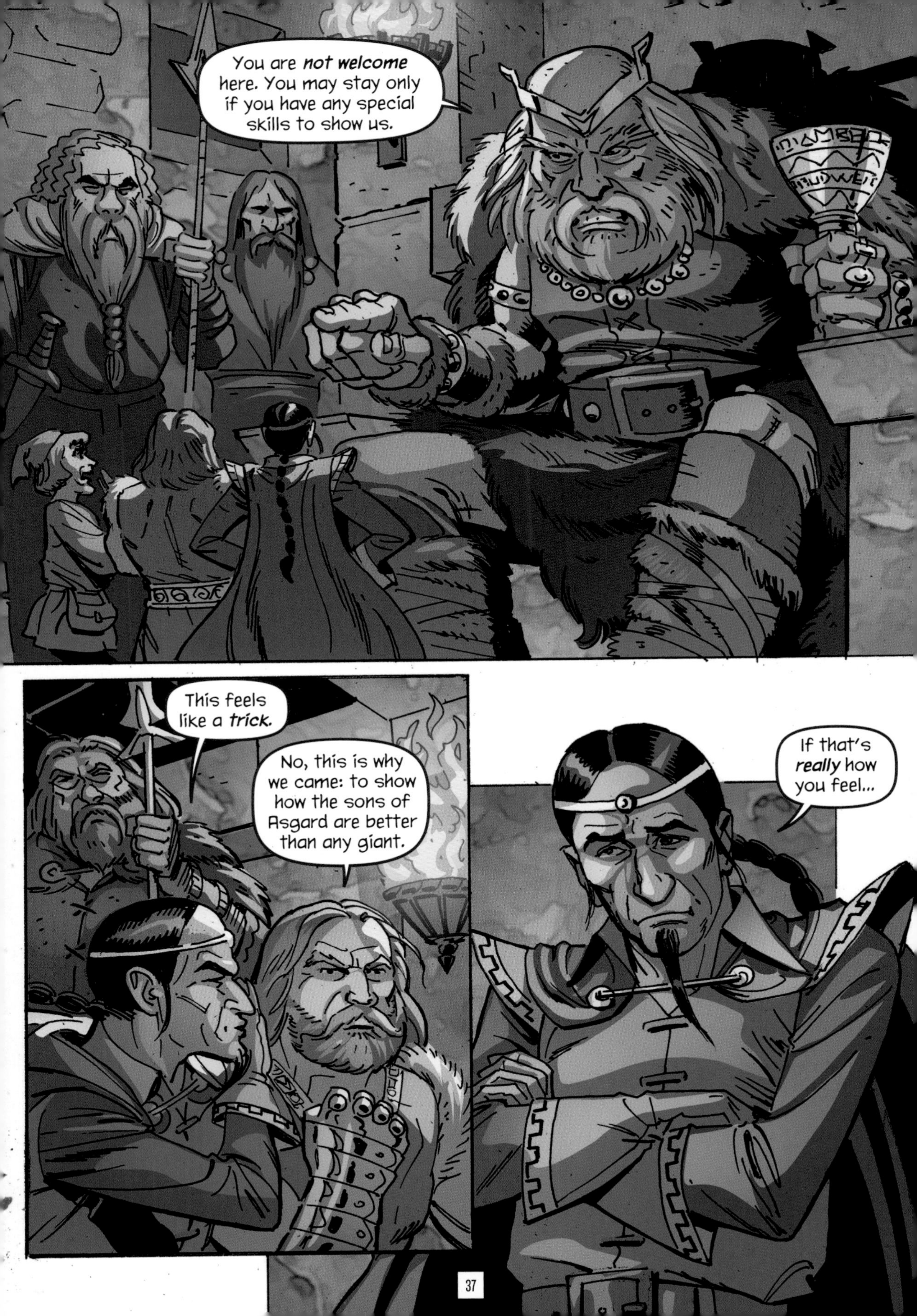
You are *not welcome* here. You may stay only if you have any special skills to show us.
This feels like a *trick*.
No, this is why we came: to show how the sons of Asgard are better than any giant.
If that's *really* how you feel...

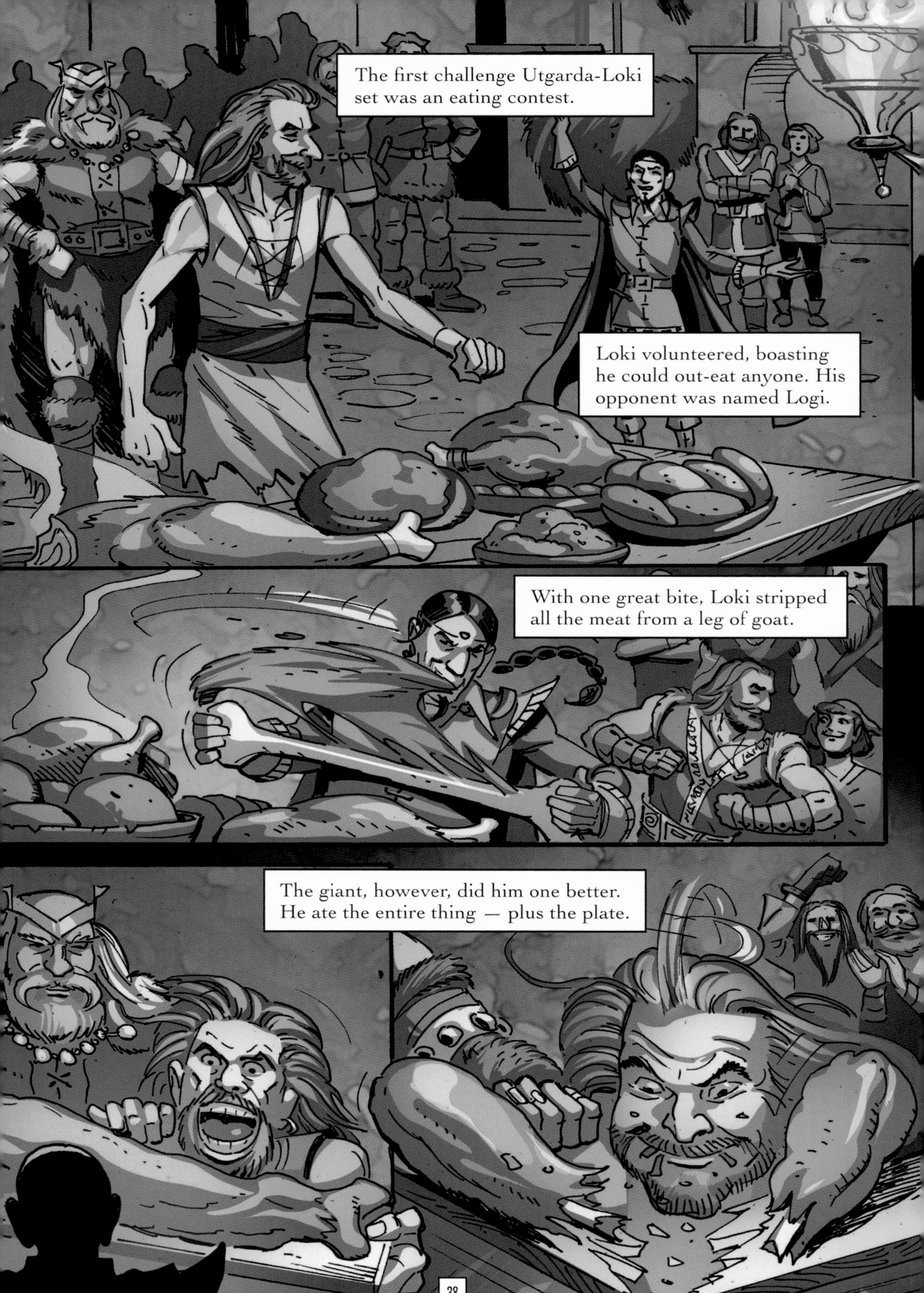
The first challenge Utgarda-Loki set was an eating contest.
Loki volunteered, boasting he could out-eat anyone. His opponent was named Logi.
With one great bite, Loki stripped all the meat from a leg of goat.
The giant, however, did him one better. He ate the entire thing — plus the plate.

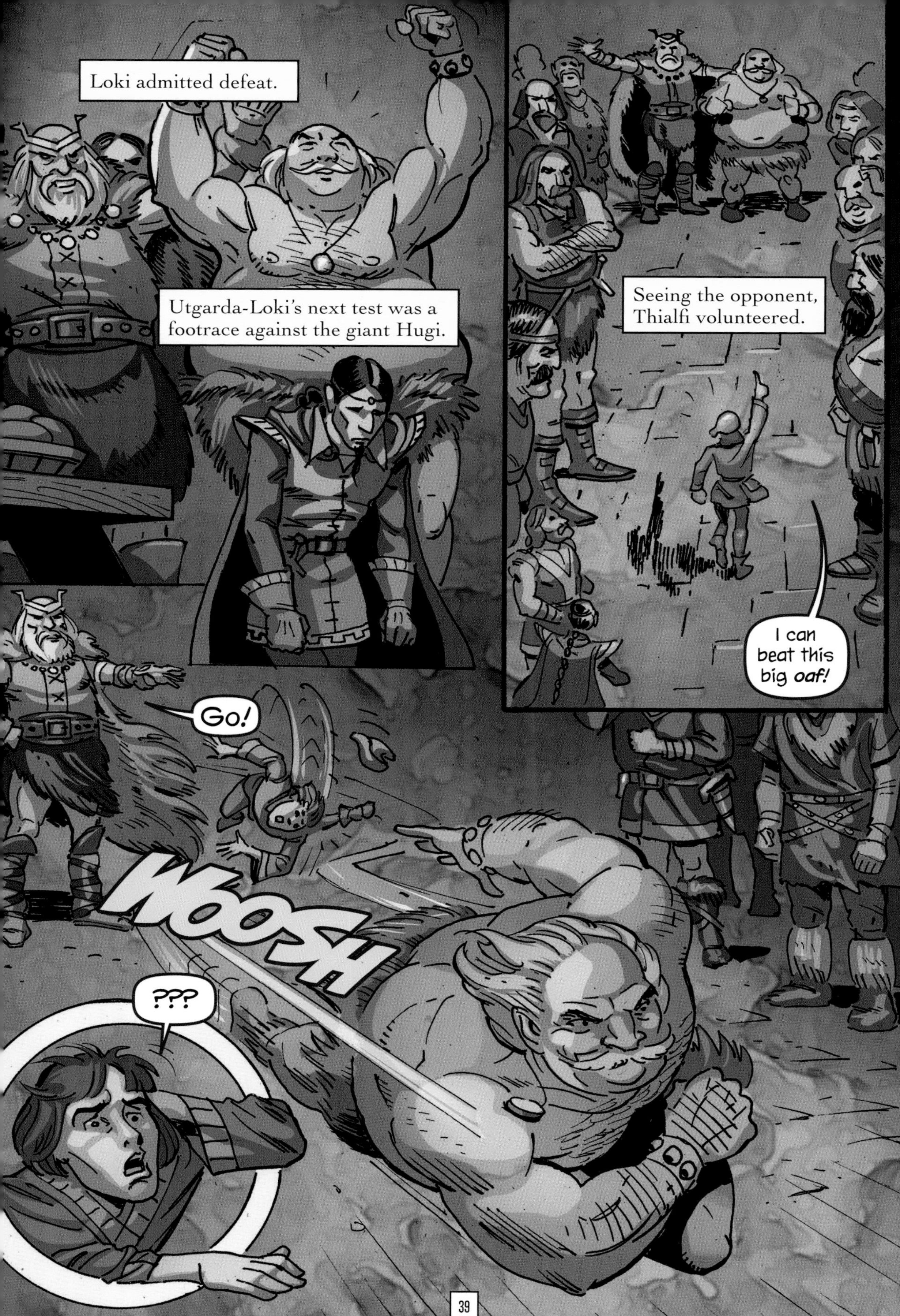
Loki admitted defeat.
Utgarda-Loki's next test was a footrace against the giant Hugi.
Seeing the opponent, Thialfi volunteered.
I can beat this big *oaf!*
Go!
WOOSH
???

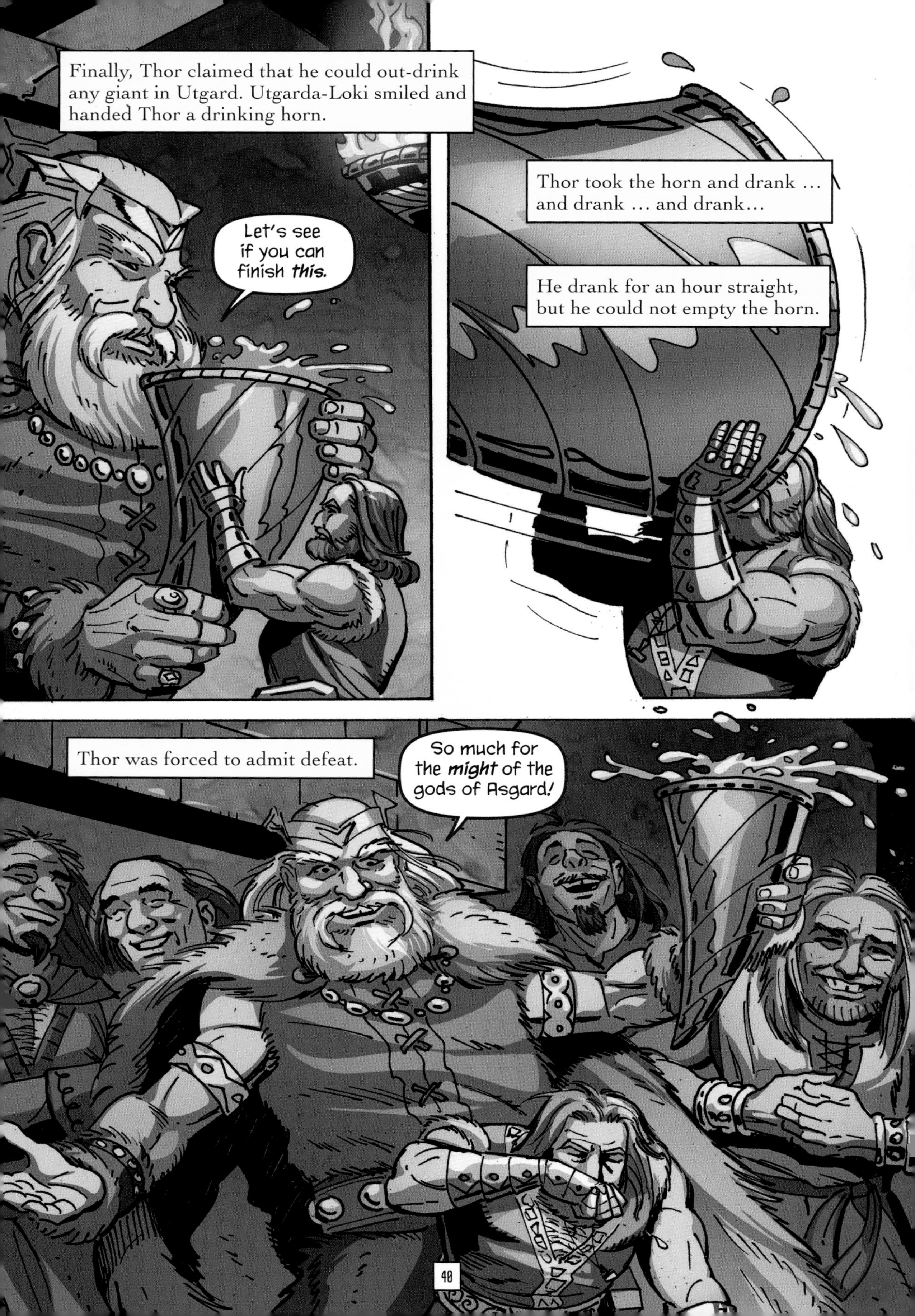
Finally, Thor claimed that he could out-drink any giant in Utgard. Utgarda-Loki smiled and handed Thor a drinking horn.
Let's see if you can finish *this.*
Thor took the horn and drank … and drank … and drank…
He drank for an hour straight, but he could not empty the horn.
Thor was forced to admit defeat.
So much for the *might* of the gods of Asgard!

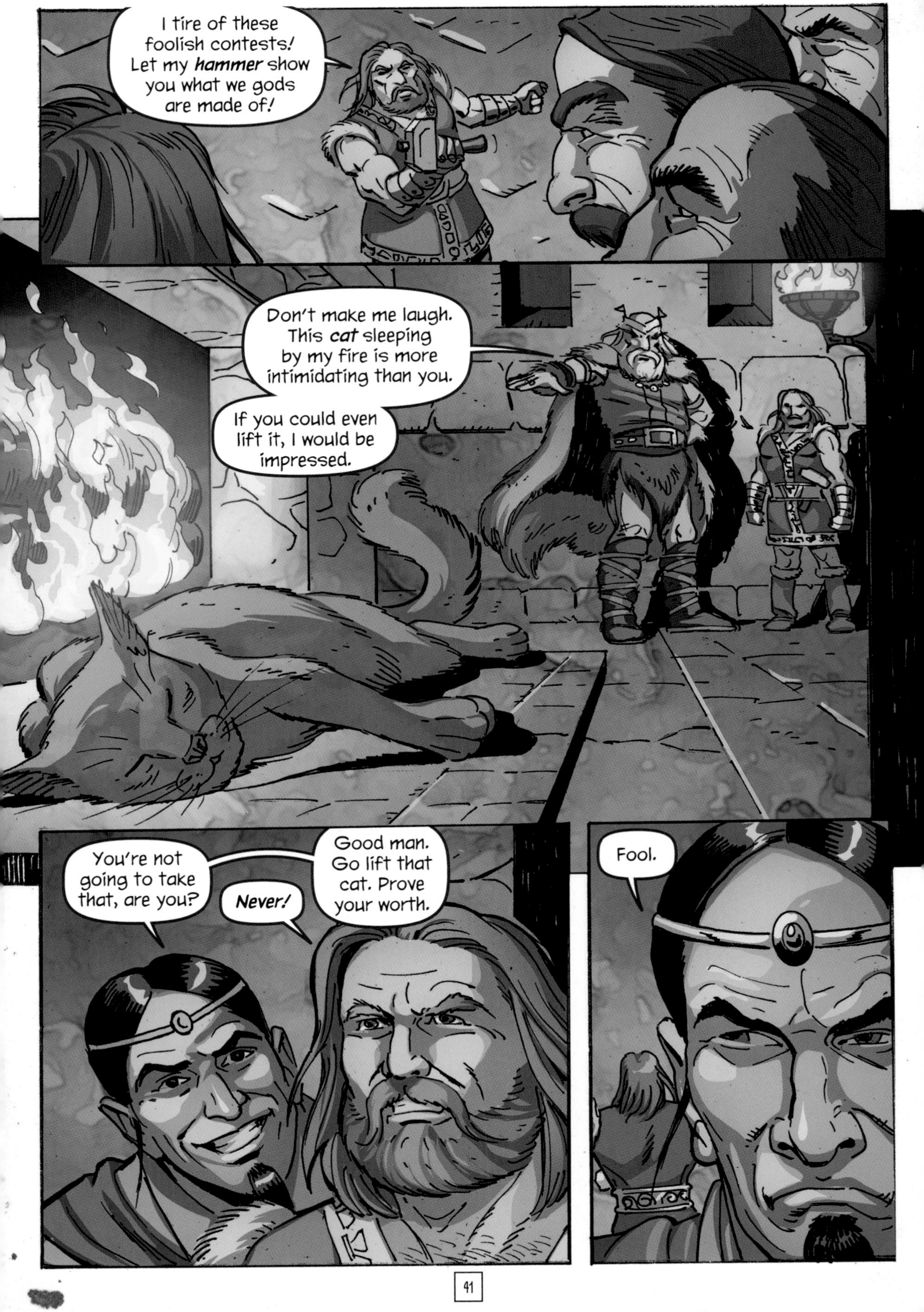
I tire of these foolish contests! Let my ***hammer*** show you what we gods are made of!
Don't make me laugh. This ***cat*** sleeping by my fire is more intimidating than you.
If you could even lift it, I would be impressed.
You're not going to take that, are you?
Never!
Good man. Go lift that cat. Prove your worth.
Fool.

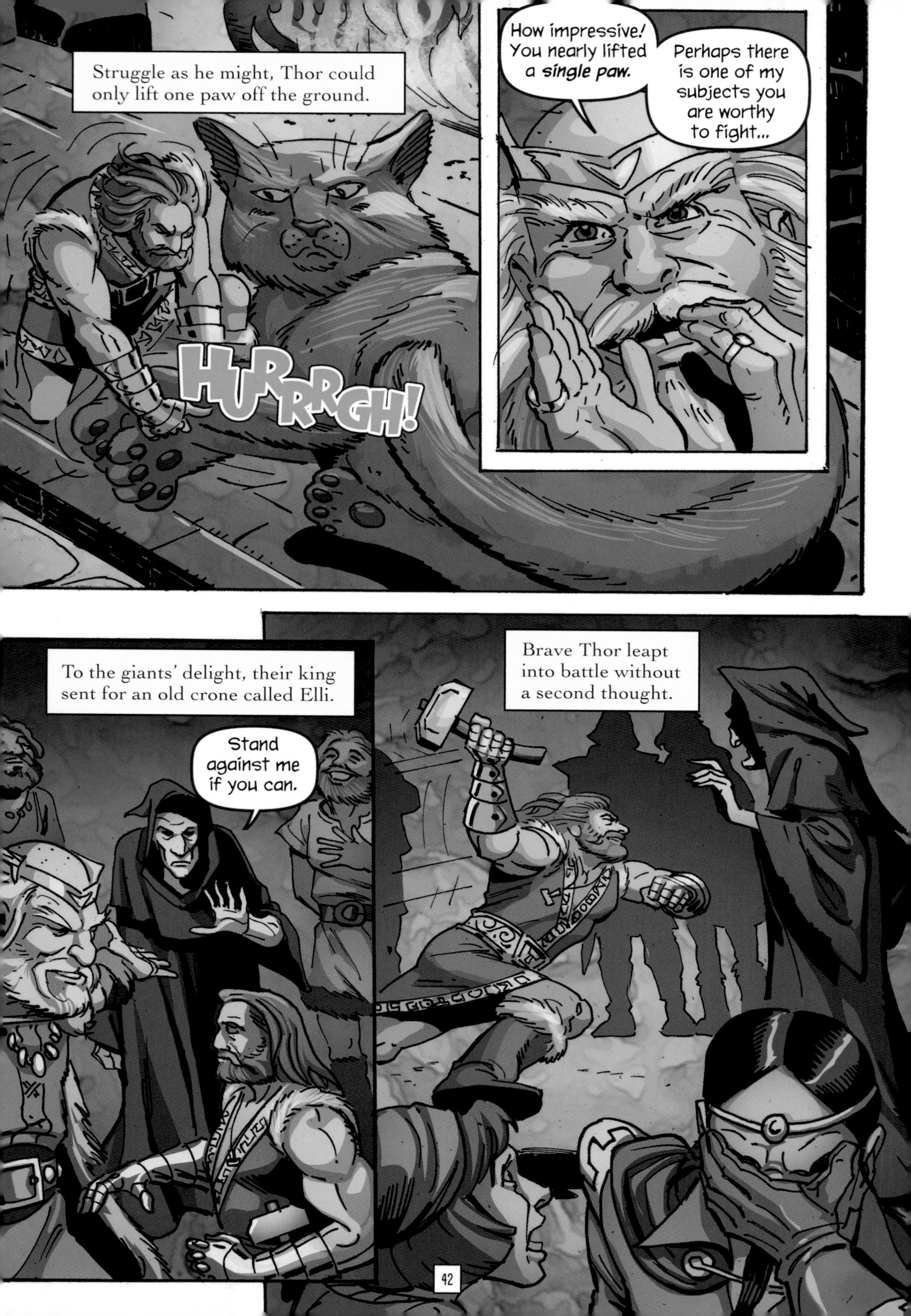

Struggle as he might, Thor could only lift one paw off the ground.
HURRRGH!
How impressive! You nearly lifted a *single paw.*
Perhaps there is one of my subjects you are worthy to fight...
To the giants' delight, their king sent for an old crone called Elli.
Stand against me if you can.
Brave Thor leapt into battle without a second thought.

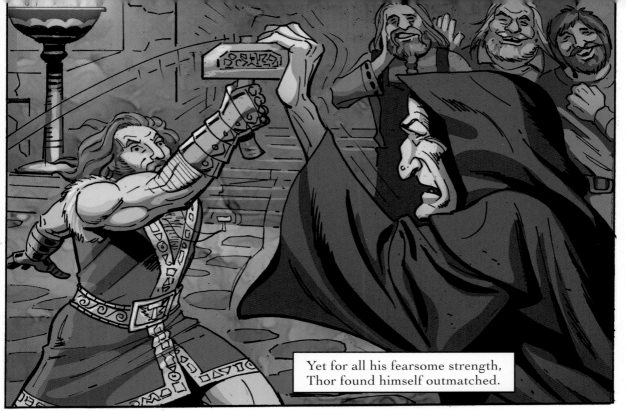

Yet for all his fearsome strength, Thor found himself outmatched.

Slowly, inevitably, the ancient one drove him to his knees.

The old woman left Thor humbled, humiliated, and defeated.

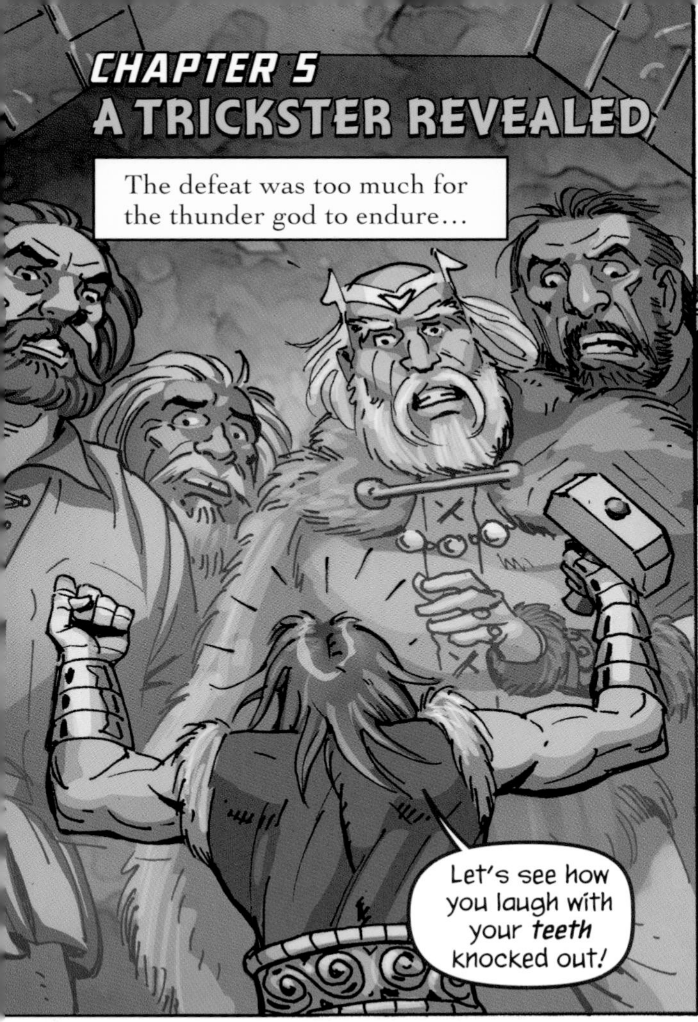
CHAPTER 5
A TRICKSTER REVEALED
The defeat was too much for the thunder god to endure…
Let's see how you laugh with your *teeth* knocked out!

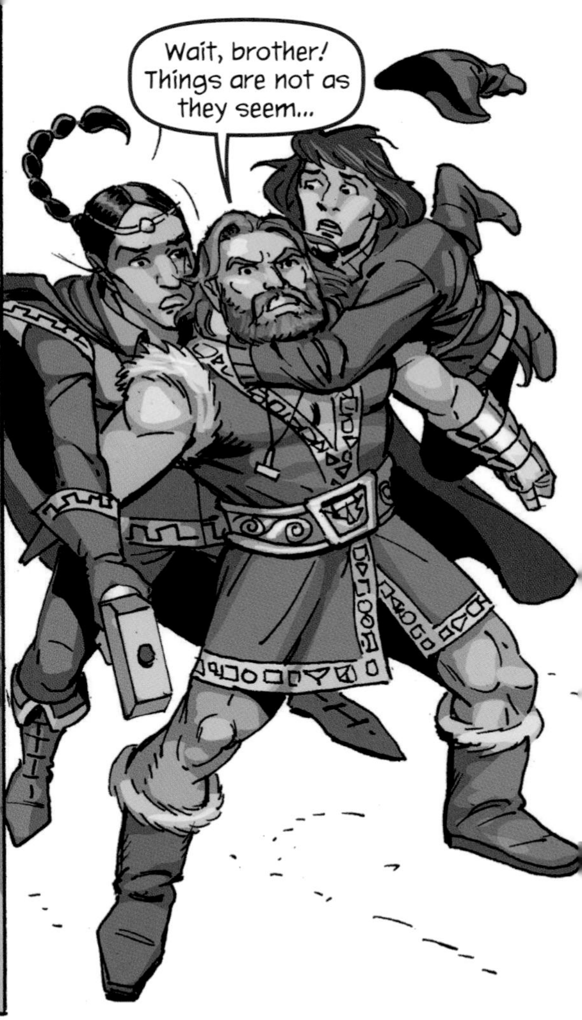
Wait, brother! Things are not as they seem...

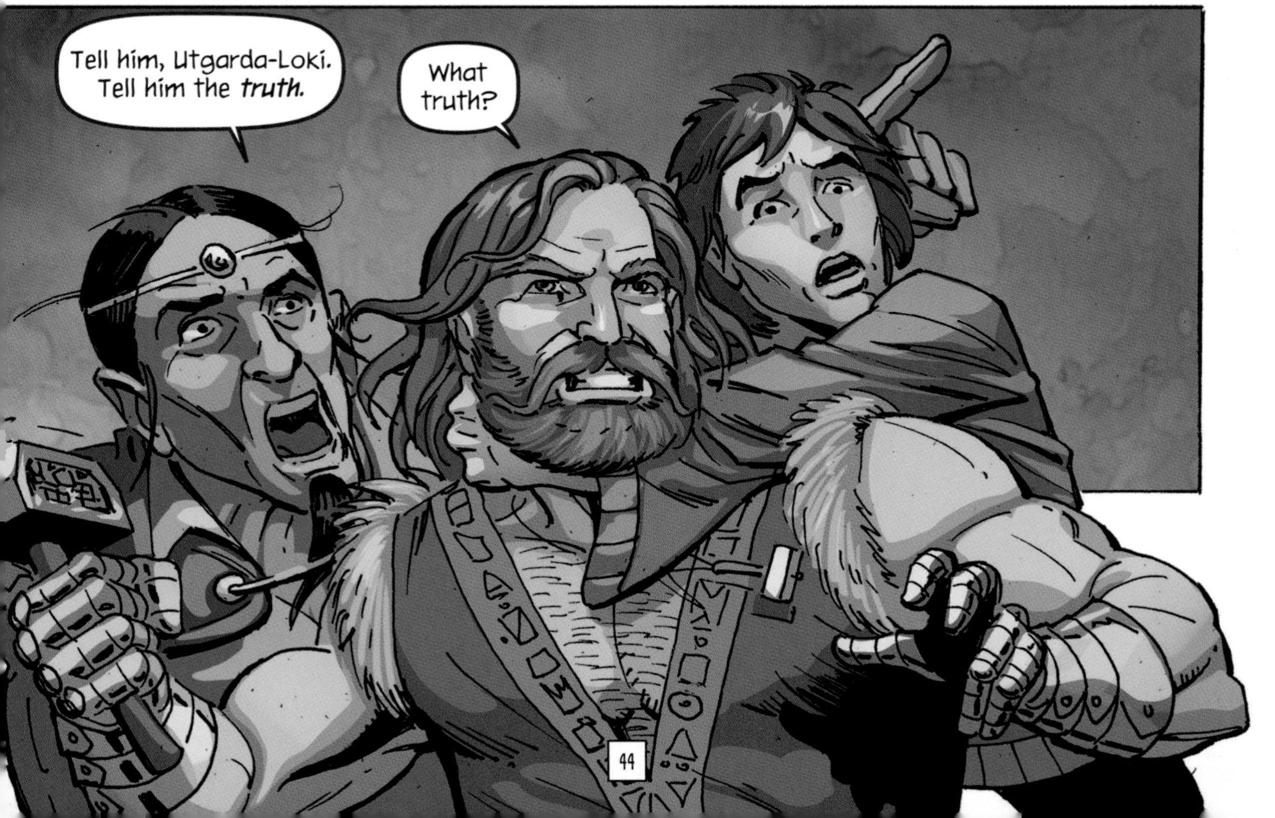
Tell him, Utgarda-Loki. Tell him the *truth.*
What truth?

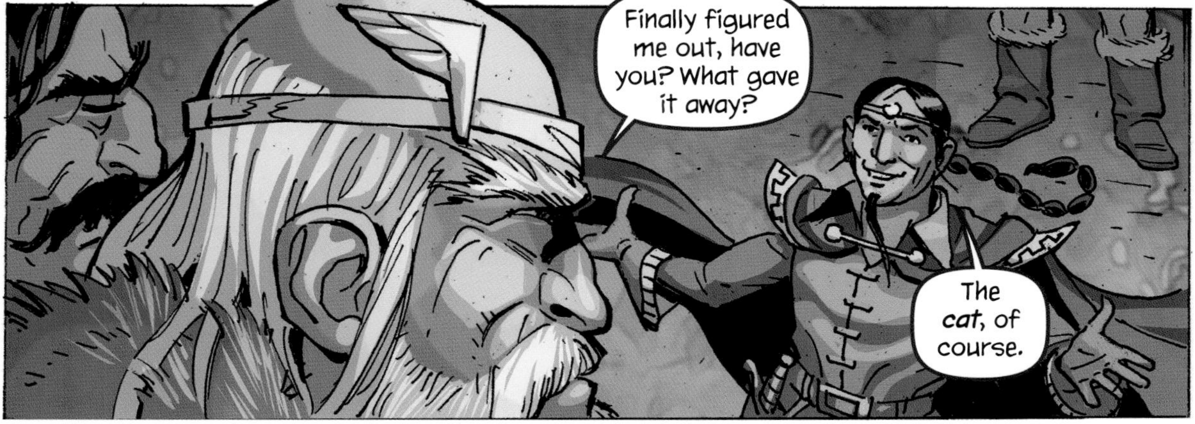
Finally figured me out, have you? What gave it away?
The *cat*, of course.

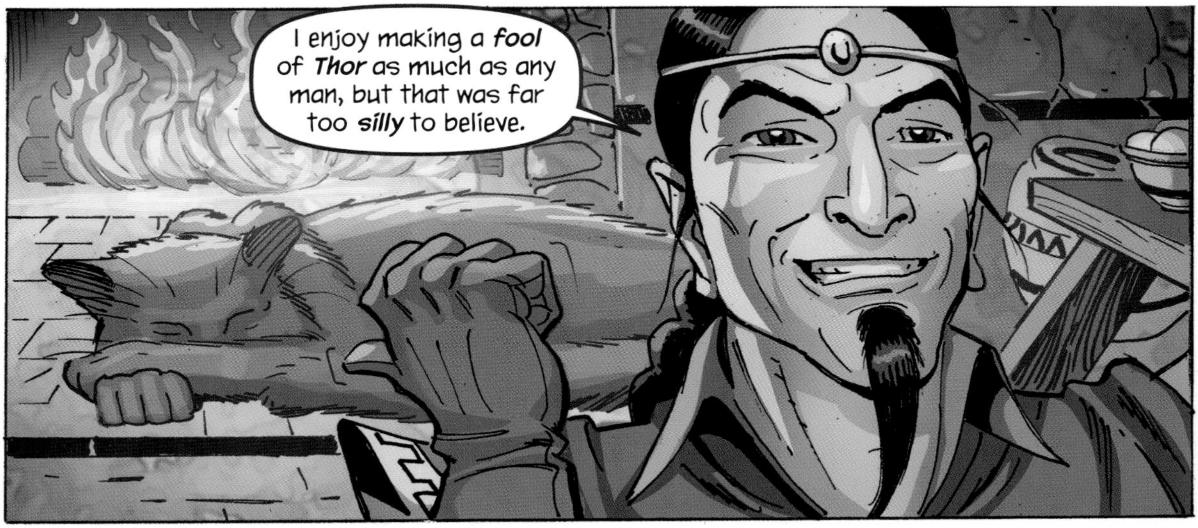
I enjoy making a *fool* of *Thor* as much as any man, but that was far too *silly* to believe.

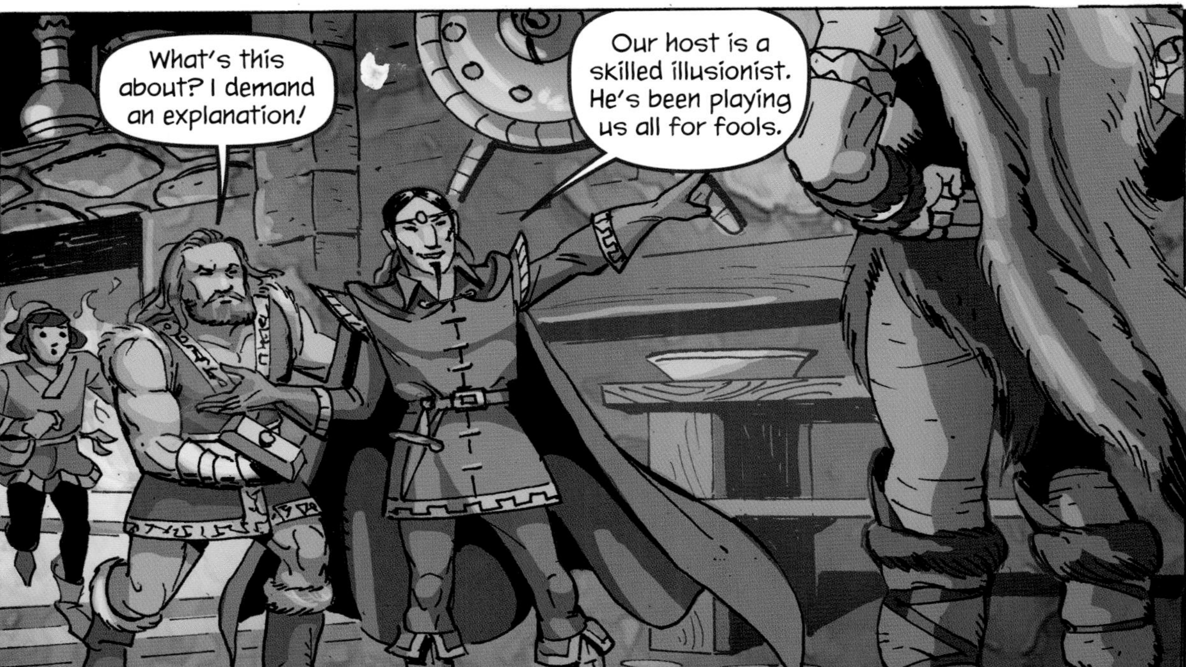
What's this about? I demand an explanation!
Our host is a skilled illusionist. He's been playing us all for fools.

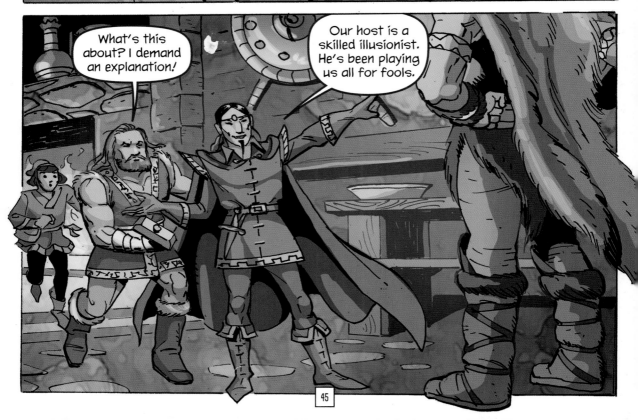

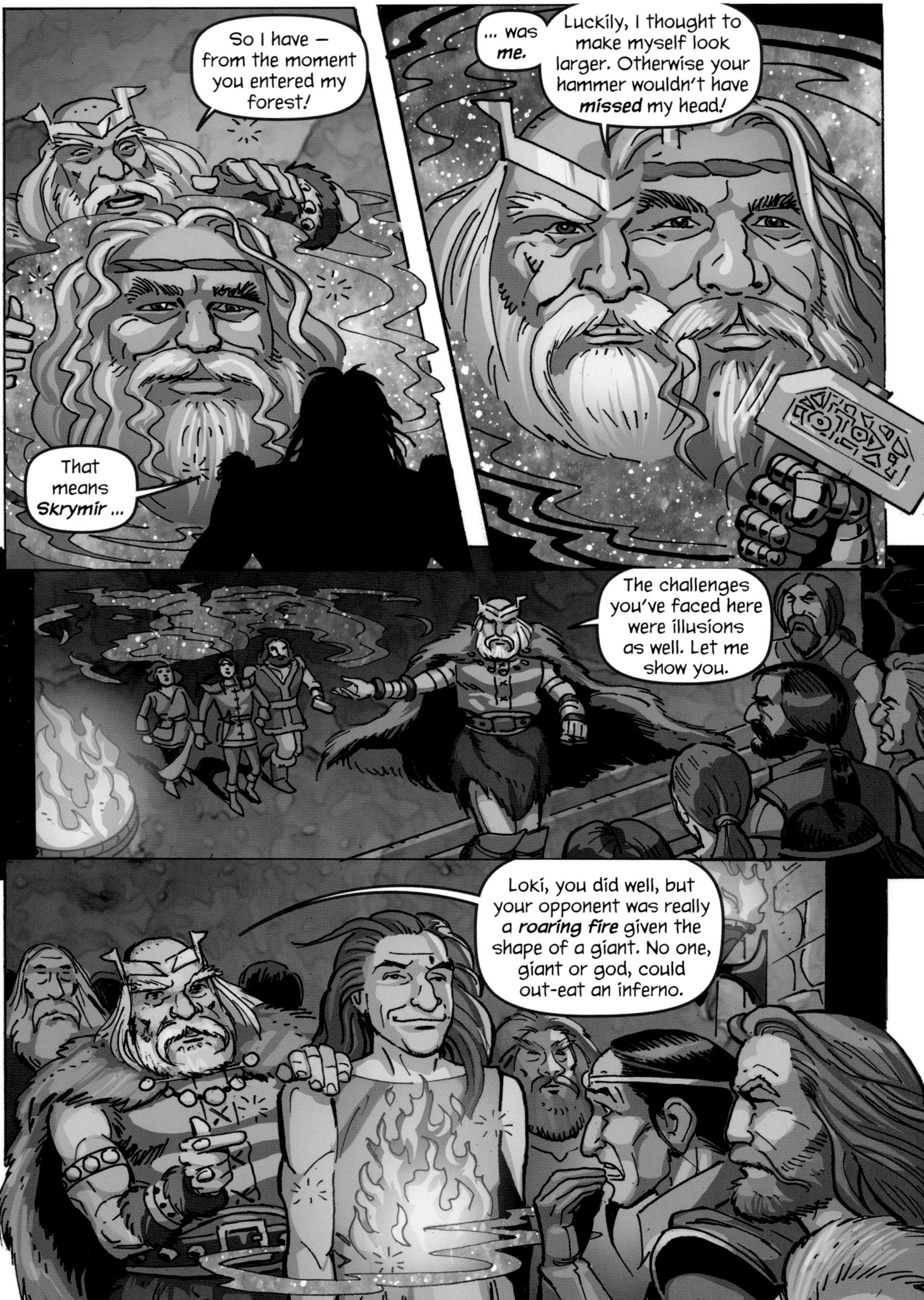
So I have — from the moment you entered my forest!
That means Skrymir ...
... was me.
Luckily, I thought to make myself look larger. Otherwise your hammer wouldn't have missed my head!
The challenges you've faced here were illusions as well. Let me show you.
Loki, you did well, but your opponent was really a roaring fire given the shape of a giant. No one, giant or god, could out-eat an inferno.

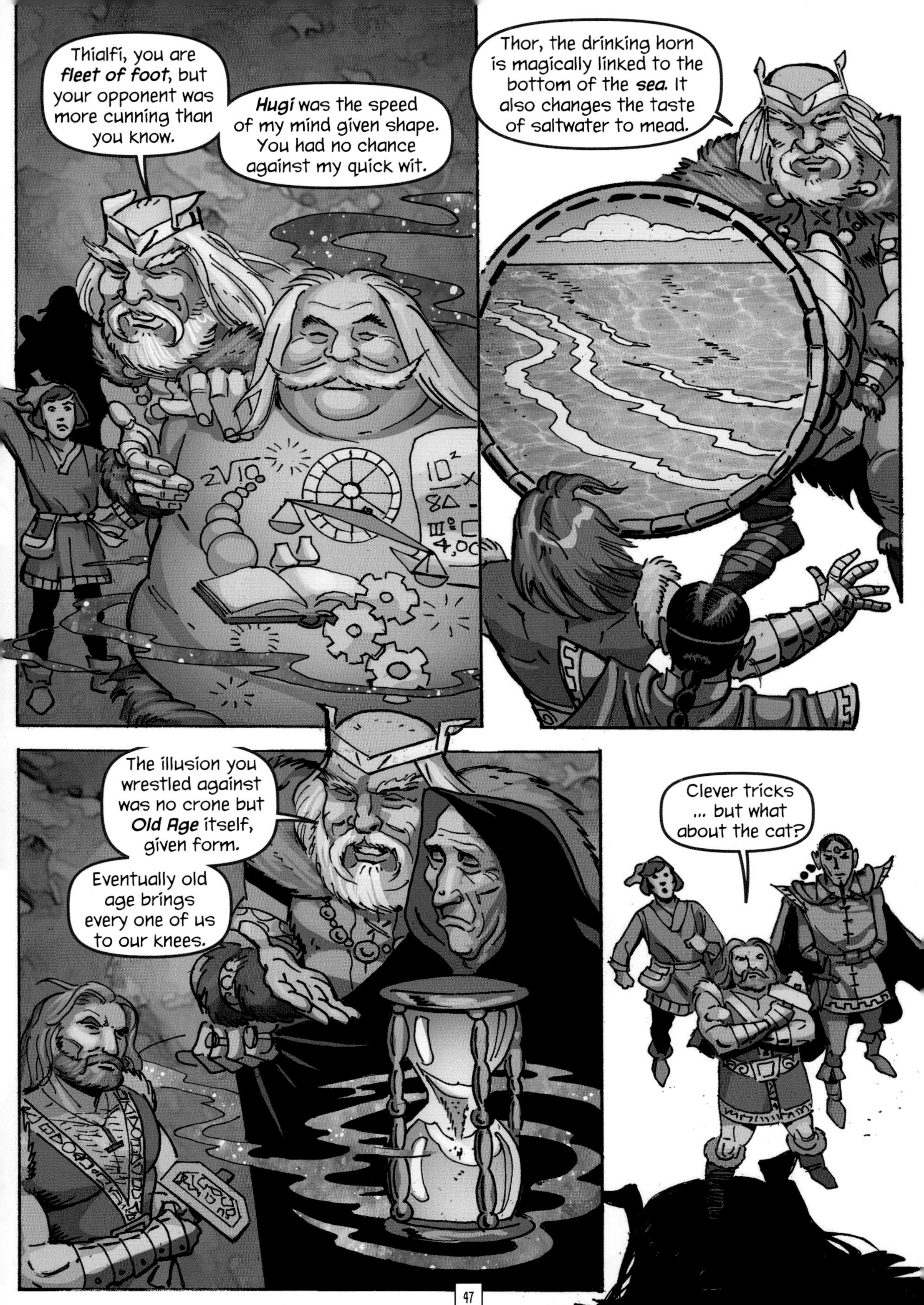
Thialfi, you are **fleet of foot**, but your opponent was more cunning than you know.
Hugi was the speed of my mind given shape. You had no chance against my quick wit.
Thor, the drinking horn is magically linked to the bottom of the **sea**. It also changes the taste of saltwater to mead.
The illusion you wrestled against was no crone but **Old Age** itself, given form.
Eventually old age brings every one of us to our knees.
Clever tricks ... but what about the cat?

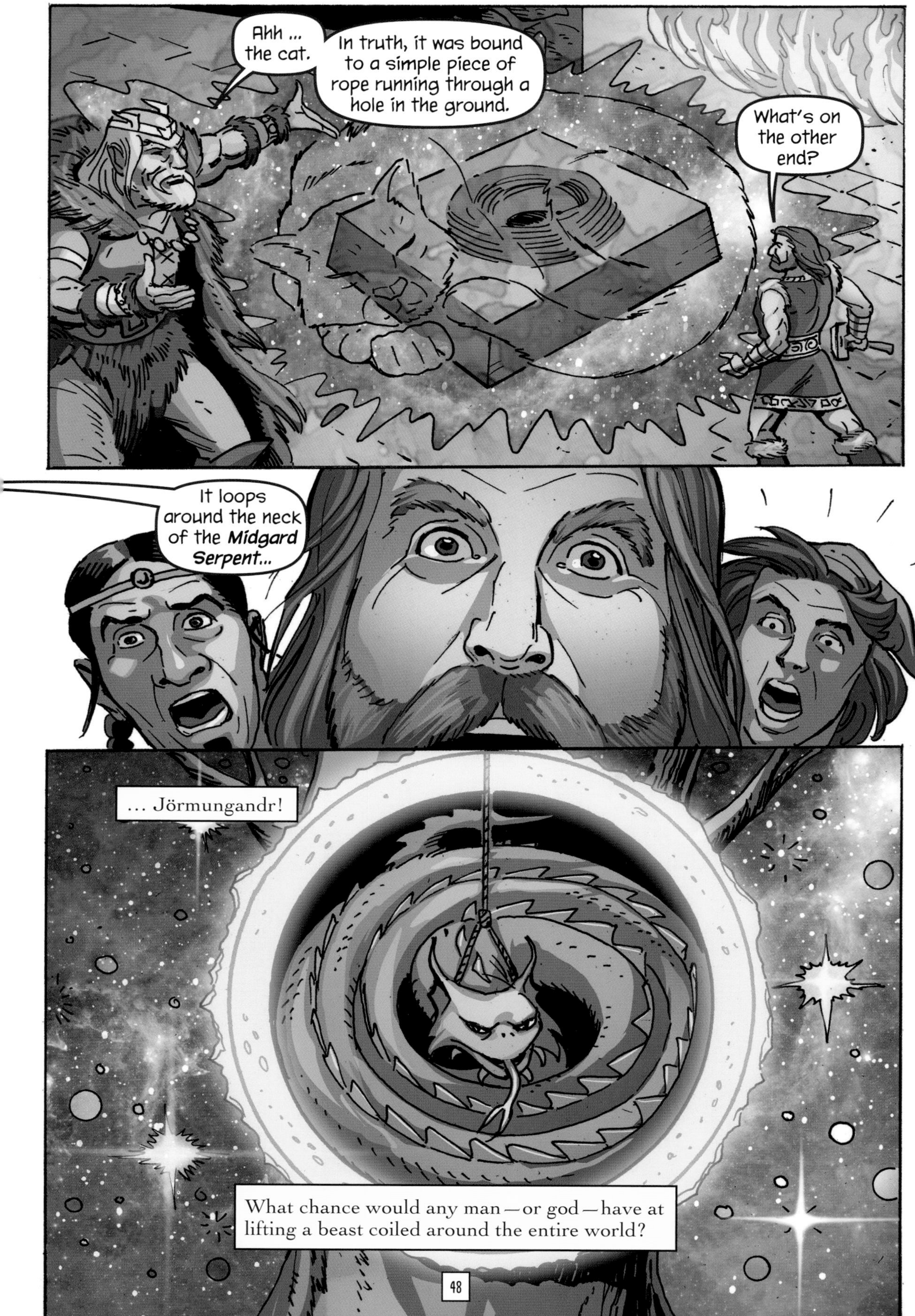

Ahh ... the cat.
In truth, it was bound to a simple piece of rope running through a hole in the ground.
What's on the other end?
It loops around the neck of the **Midgard Serpent**...
... Jörmungandr!
What chance would any man—or god—have at lifting a beast coiled around the entire world?

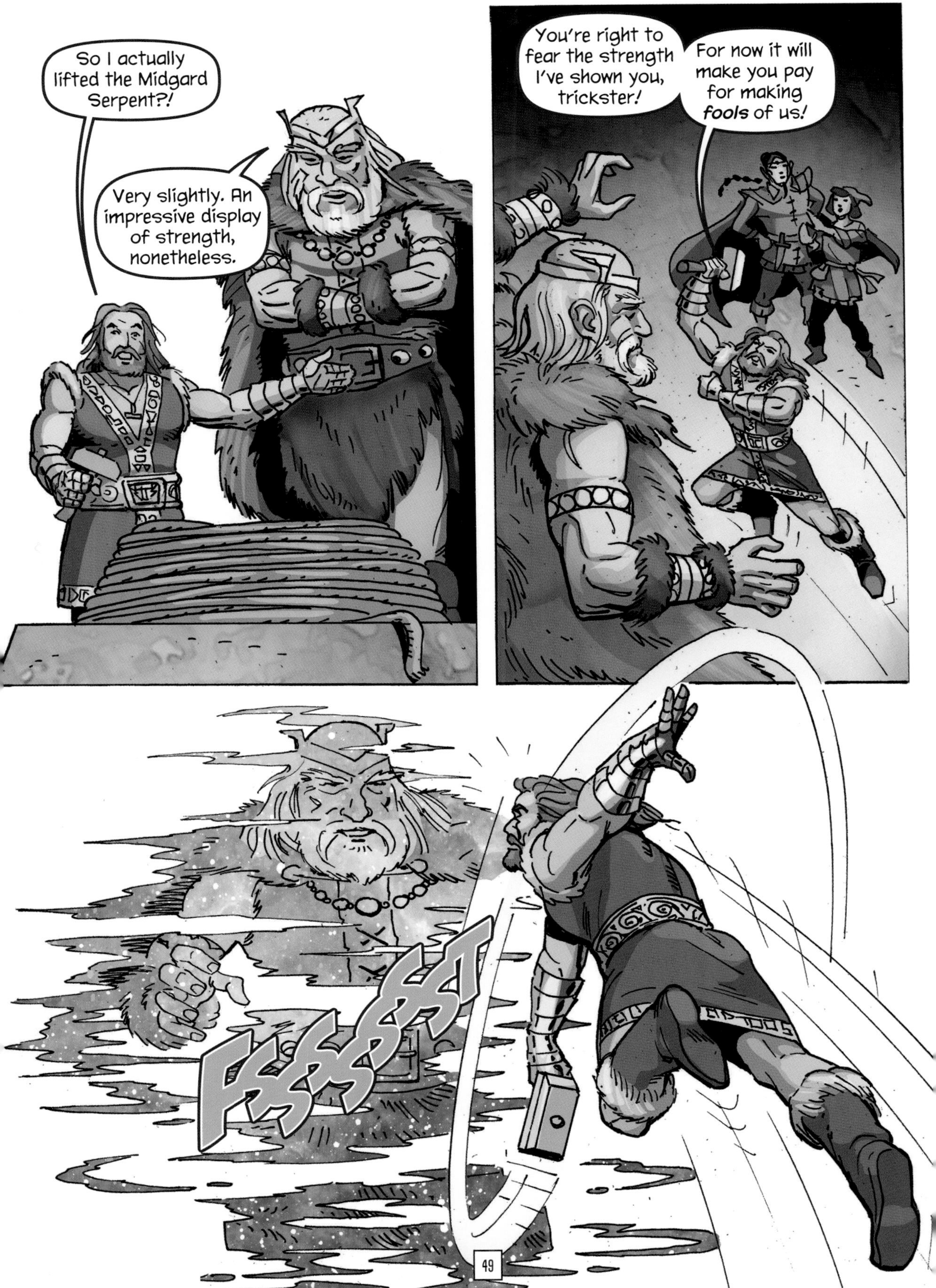
So I actually lifted the Midgard Serpent?!
Very slightly. An impressive display of strength, nonetheless.
You're right to fear the strength I've shown you, trickster!
For now it will make you pay for making fools of us!
FSSSSST

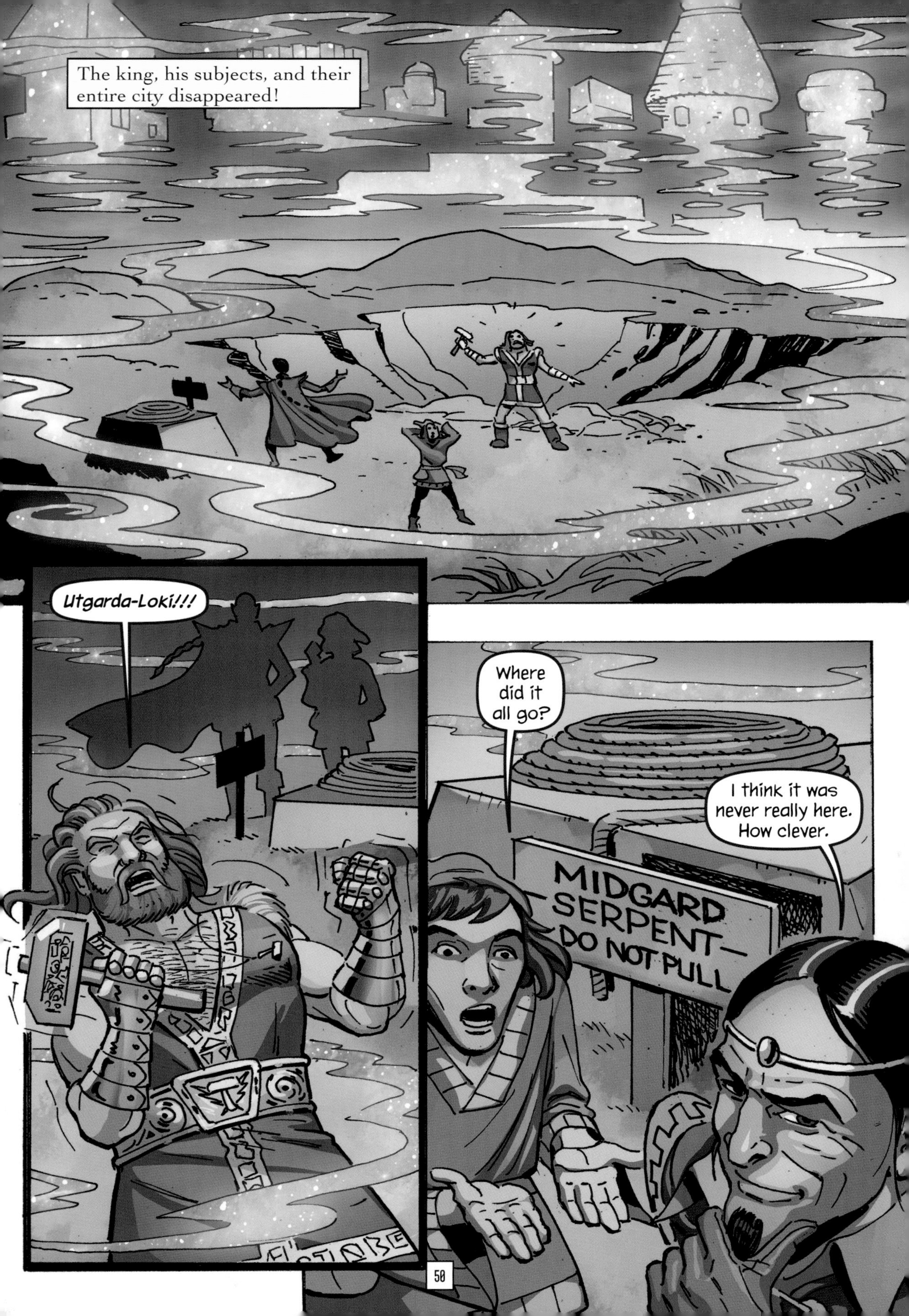
The king, his subjects, and their entire city disappeared!
Utgarda-Loki!!!
Where did it all go?
I think it was never really here. How clever.
MIDGARD SERPENT DO NOT PULL

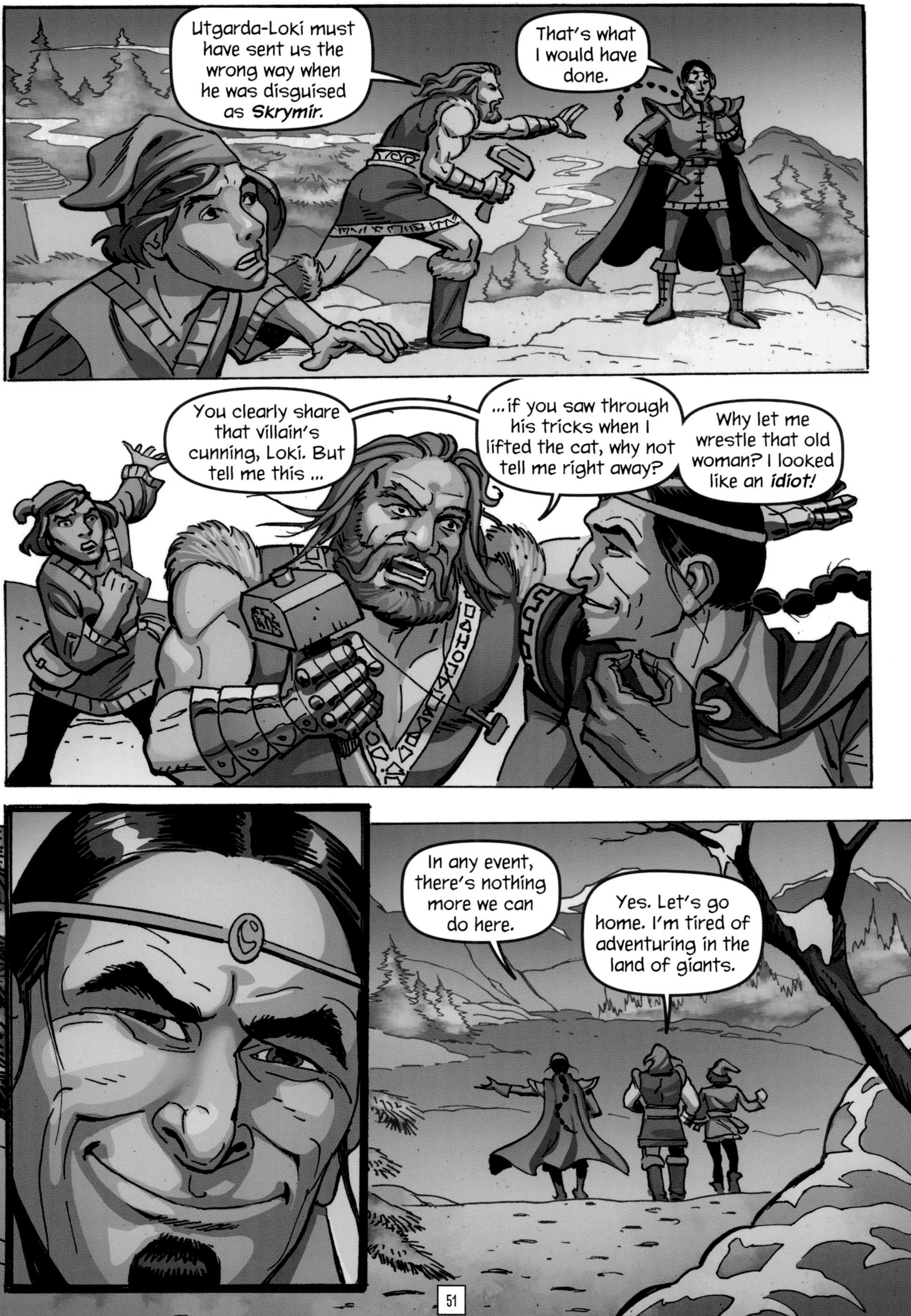

Utgarda-Loki must have sent us the wrong way when he was disguised as **Skrymir**.
That's what I would have done.
You clearly share that villain's cunning, Loki. But tell me this ...
...if you saw through his tricks when I lifted the cat, why not tell me right away?
Why let me wrestle that old woman? I looked like an *idiot!*
In any event, there's nothing more we can do here.
Yes. Let's go home. I'm tired of adventuring in the land of giants.

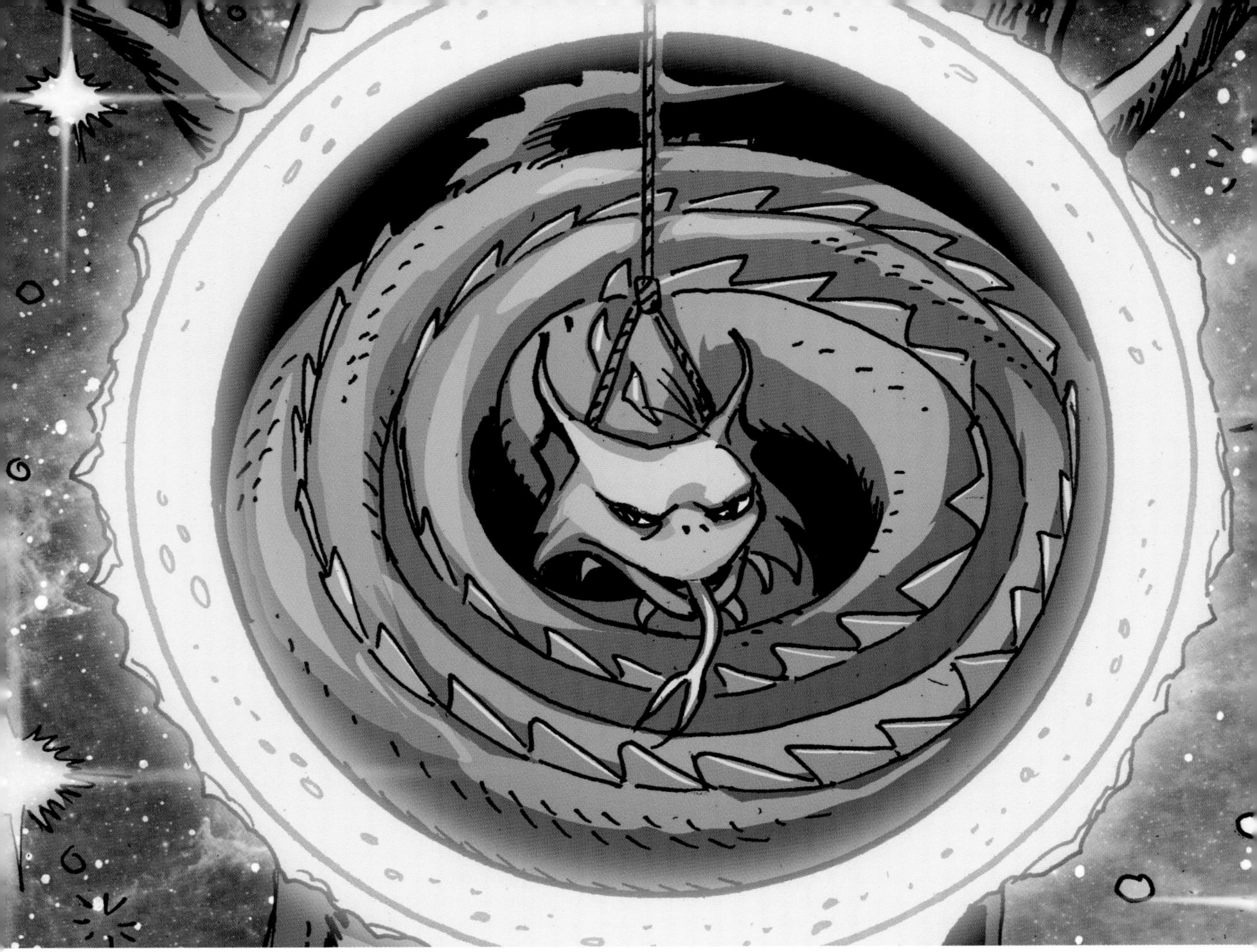

ABOUT THE RETELLING AUTHOR AND ARTISTS

Carl Bowen is a father, husband, and writer living in Lawrenceville, Georgia, by way of Alexandria, Louisiana, and RAF Alconbury in Cambridgeshire, England.

His works include graphic novel retellings of classic sci-fi tales, original comics set in the world of freestyle BMX riding and high school football, and a far-out twist on the classic "Jack and the Beanstalk" story. He's also the author of the Firestormers series and the *Kirkus* star-reviewed Shadow Squadron series.

As of this writing, Carl has yet to try fighting giants with a magical war hammer.

Tod Smith is a self-employed illustrator and a graduate of the Joe Kubert School of Cartooning and Graphic Art. He has illustrated a wide variety of books, including work for Marvel Comics. He currently lives in Hartford, Connecticut.

Rex Lokus has been working in the comics industry for more than 10 years. Hired by companies such as Marvel, DC Comics, Capstone, Wizuale (Poland), and FuryLion Studios (Russia). He has also worked on various independent projects.

GLOSSARY

Aesir (AY-zir)—the name given to the collection of gods and goddesses found in the ancient Norse religion

chariot (CHAYR-ee-uht)—a light, two-wheeled cart

drinking horn (DRINK-ing HOHRN)—a drinking vessel made from the hollowed out horn of a large animal

humiliate (hyoo-MIHL-ee-ayt)—to make someone look or feel foolish or embarrassed

illusion (i-LOO-shuhn)—something that appears to be real but isn't

Jötunheim (YOH-toon-heym)—the land of the giants in ancient Norse mythology

marrow (MA-roh)—the soft substance inside bones that is used to make blood cells

mead (MEED)—a wine-like drink made from water, honey, malt, and yeast

Midgard (MID-gahrd)—the land of humankind in ancient Norse mythology

mortal (MOR-tul)—unable to live forever

musty (MUHSS-tee)—smelling of dampness, decay, or mold

volunteer (vol-uhn-TIHR)—to offer to do something

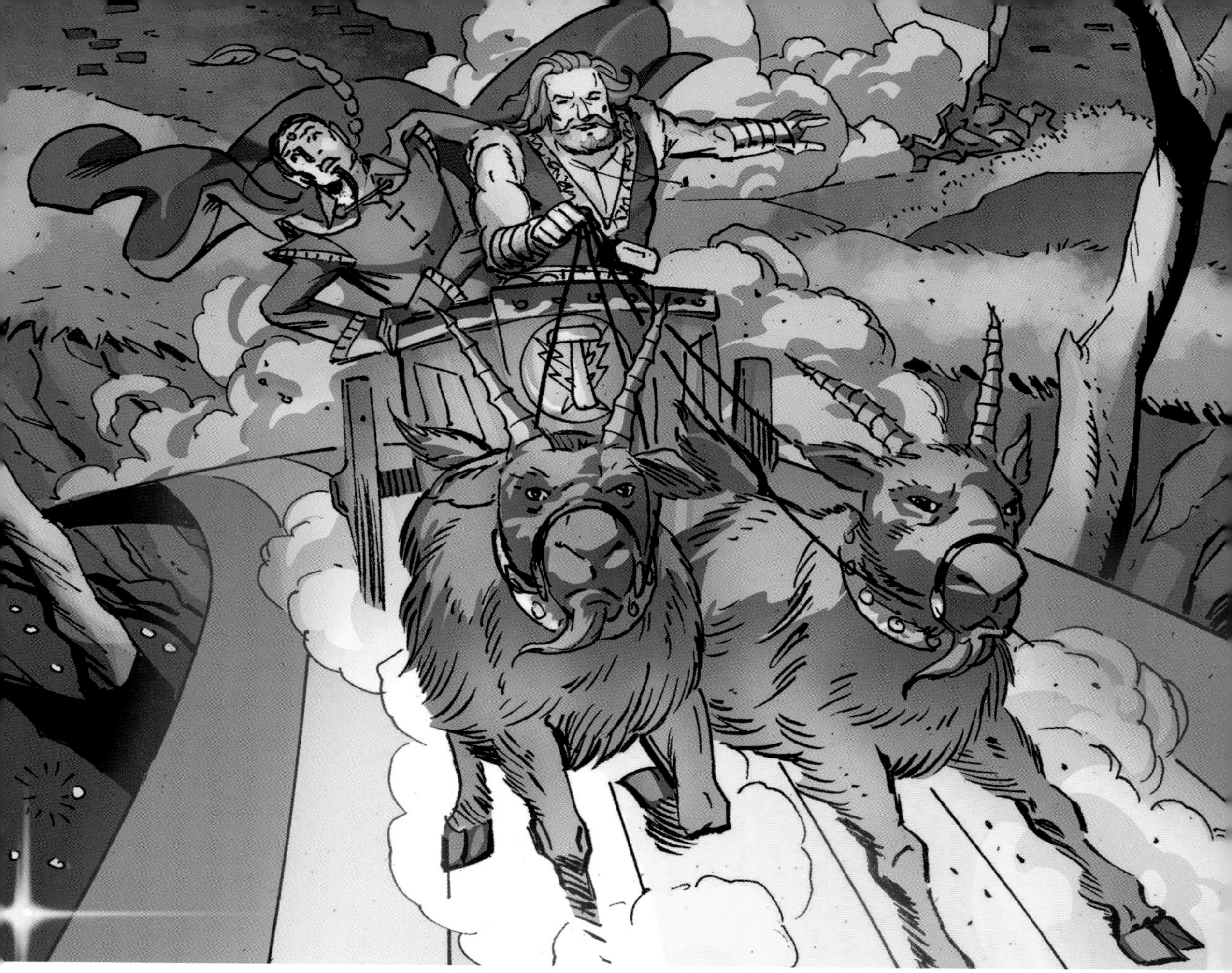

DISCUSSION QUESTIONS

1. When Thor says he wants to travel to the land of the giants, Odin tells him that Loki must travel with him. Why do you think Odin wanted Loki to go with Thor?

2. After the feast at Egil's house, Loki tricked Thialfi into breaking one of the goats' leg bones and eating the marrow. Why do you think Loki tricked the young man? What would you do in Thialfi's place?

3. Thor, Loki, and Thialfi all failed in the challenges given to them by Utgarda-Loki. Why do you think they were easily fooled by the giant king's illusions?

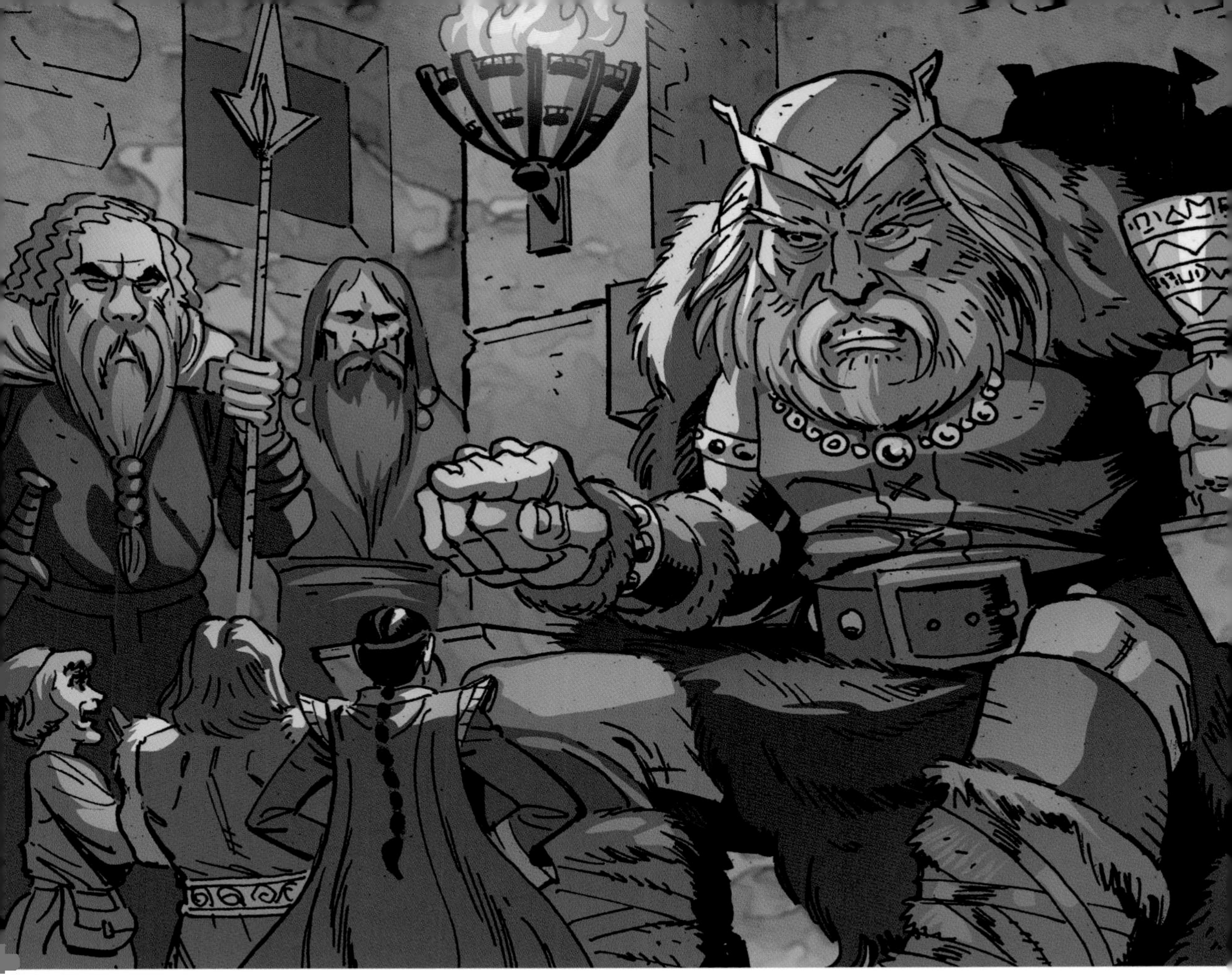

WRITING PROMPTS

1. Throughout the story Loki pokes fun at Thor and enjoys tricking him into doing foolish things. Has anyone ever tried to trick you into doing something foolish? What did you do about it? Write down what happened and how you reacted to the situation.

2. When Thor faced the colossal giant Skrymir, he was frightened but still showed great bravery. Write about a time when you were scared to do something but found the courage to do it anyway.

3. The main characters faced several challenges that tested their strength, speed, and skill. Think about other types of challenges Thor and Loki could do. Write a short story describing how they would perform in those contests.

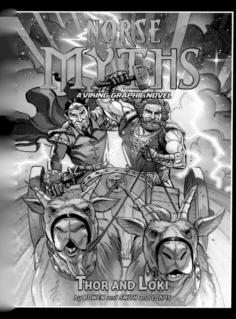

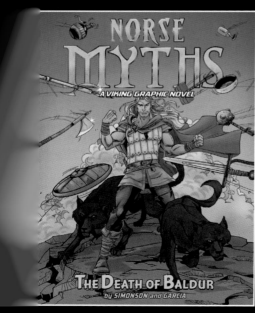
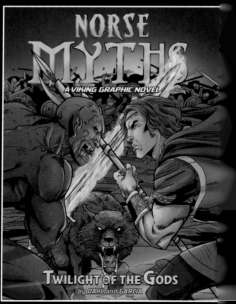